ZIEGLER SHOOK HIS HEAD SADLY,

then nodded toward the guard, who pulled Carter's baby finger the rest of the way back until it popped, the breaking bone sending a huge bolt of pain through the back of Carter's head . . . almost as if he had received a massive electric shock.

"There are nine fingers remaining. Then the toes. And if all else fails, there are interesting things to be done with your anus, or perhaps even your testicles." Ziegler chuckled.

The guard moved to Carter's ring finger.

"I'll tell you," Carter shouted. "Christ, it's not worth this . . ."

NICK CARTER IS IT!

"Nick Carter out-Bonds James Bond."
—Buffalo Evening News

"Nick Carter is America's #1 espionage agent."
—Variety

"Nick Carter is razor-sharp suspense."
—King Features

"Nick Carter is extraordinarily big."
—Bestsellers

"Nick Carter has attracted an army of addicted readers . . . the books are fast, have plenty of action and just the right degree of sex . . . Nick Carter is the American James Bond, suave, sophisticated, a killer with both the ladies and the enemy."
—The New York Times

FROM THE NICK CARTER
KILLMASTER SERIES

NICK CARTER

KILLMASTER

EARTHFIRE NORTH

CHARTER BOOKS, NEW YORK

EARTHFIRE NORTH

A Charter Book/published by arrangement with
The Condé Nast Publications, Inc.

PRINTING HISTORY
Charter Original/November 1983

Charter Books are published by The Berkley Publishing Group,
200 Madison Avenue, New York, N.Y. 10016
PRINTED IN THE UNITED STATES OF AMERICA

*Dedicated to the men of the
Secret Services of the United
States of America*

EARTHFIRE NORTH

PROLOGUE

Dr. Lydia Coatsworth strode into her small office in the geology lab at the University of Iceland carrying a large pile of photographs. She cleared the coffee cups, files, and other paraphernalia from the desk top and arranged the glossy prints in rows, starting in the upper left-hand corner and working her way down.

The photos were bizarre: the same shot over and over of a craggy finger of rock protruding from what looked to be the mouth of the River Styx, a roiling section of seawater from which mist and vapor poured like steam from a kettle. Occasionally, as she dealt them out, she'd squint down at one of them under the light, tap her finger making note of it, then go on. The experiment was almost completed, she told herself, the last piece of evidence about to fall into place. The conclusion inevitable but impossible, not to be believed.

When she finished, she had six rows of photos, sixty to a row, two complete time-lapse sequences taken one-a-second for three minutes, each sequence twenty-four hours apart. She took a set of calipers from the drawer and, with the deliberate slowness of an experienced scientist, began to take measurements of images in each photo, noting her results in a thick notebook.

The roiling water and steam were the surface phenomena of a volcanic fissure that had opened up in the ocean floor

1

several hundred yards off the coast. It had been discovered only a week earlier, the captain of the passing trawler reporting the incident to the Department of Fisheries, which in turn passed it on to the university for further study.

Dr. Coatsworth had leaped at the opportunity to study this new activity. She was a visitor to Iceland, part of a faculty exchange program with the Massachusetts Institute of Technology, and saw in the new volcano a chance to familiarize herself with the unique structure of Icelandic geology. She made it her pet project from the beginning, attacking it with characteristic thoroughness. She took hourly temperature readings at various depths to build heat gradient charts, took seismographic readings to determine the size of the opening and the amount and direction of the lava flow, and chemical analyses of the steam to see if it compared with other volcanic hot spots in and around Iceland.

It was this last series of tests that began to point to something wrong, terribly wrong: so wrong it sent a tremor through the terra firma of her geological knowledge.

Among the trace chemicals mentioned in the lab report was a polymer—di-chloridepolyethanol—a man-made constituent of certain types of anticorrosive plastic pipe joints used in oil production and occasionally to transport live steam. It was never known to occur in nature.

The results were rechecked, of course. There was no mistake. The dcp was definitely in the steam, not in the testing equipment. And Lydia Coatsworth was forced to wonder what the true source of this fissure was.

Then other evidence surfaced. The fissure had a dormant period during which the eruption ceased altogether. It lasted roughly eight hours, from 2340 until 0815, and was so exact she could set her watch by it. Too exact. It was almost as though someone were turning a switch off and on.

Two nights ago she had guided a small rowboat through the churning water, steam, and mist to a tiny rock in the center of the activity, where she set up a camera. She pointed the lens at another rock a dozen yards away, then set the time-lapse trigger for one shot every second for a total of three minutes bracketed around 2340 and again around 0815. Then she'd returned to her car to wait. In the morning she rowed out, collected the film, then rushed back to the lab to develop and analyze it.

By measuring the fluctuations of the height of the water on certain areas of the rock, she was able to determine when the eruption began and ended. From this, two facts emerged. First, the entire cycle was not a gradual process, such as usually occurred in nature; the eruption stopped precisely at 2341:23 and began again at 0815:56. And second, the start-up was not accompanied by a constant surge; there was a hesitation in the water flow, such as when a hydraulic pump clears itself, then reprimes.

The conclusion was being forced on her, yet it seemed too fantastic to believe. Better to wait, she thought. Better to corroborate the evidence.

The previous night she'd once again dared the dangers of froth and mist aboard the small boat. She'd taken her photographs and returned, spending an hour in the darkroom. Now, as she pored over them, she tried very hard to be objective about what she was seeing, not letting the weight of past evidence influence her findings. But as she took her measurements and made her tables of differences in water level, her heart beat faster and her tongue clicked noisily in the dryness of her mouth.

The hesitation at the beginning of the cycle was still there. Just as it had been the night before. There was no mistaking it. The eruption ceased at exactly the same time both nights, then started again as if on cue, to the very second. The chances of something like this happening naturally were trillions to one. There was no way to escape the conclusion this time. The fissure was being operated mechanically. But by whom? And why?

She stepped to the window and stared out at the treeless landscape of southern Iceland. In all respects except one— the timing—the fissure and the volcanic release of steam could have been natural. All but the timing, that is, she corrected herself, *and* the evidence of the polymer.

Her hands were shaking. She lit a cigarette, the action calming her somewhat. A large portion of the population of Iceland, which numbered almost a quarter of a million, were dependent for their heat and hot water on geothermal sources. Years ago, natural steam jets had been tapped in a lava field south of Reykjavik, the capital city. Since then, the island had enjoyed abundant, pollution-free energy at a very cheap rate. But in the last week, since this new fissure had opened, the level and intensity of the steam had decreased dramatically. Petur Tomasson, a colleague in her department at the university, had been asked by the government to investigate this latest fluctuation. There had been no official announcement, of course; such fluctuations, although not common, were certainly not rare. So far, all they had were theories. Except now for this. . . .

The exactness with which the eruption occurred, the existence of the polymer—which strongly suggested a man-made pipeline—and the sudden decrease in the steam jets outside Reykjavik were all too much of a mysterious coincidence for her. Obviously someone was diverting water and steam from the city's supply and sending it through the fissure in the ocean. But who? And why?

Whoever it was had vast resources. Pipelines had to be dug, a pumping station erected. It had to have taken extensive planning and engineering as well as the cooperation of hundreds of people. How had something like this been kept under wraps in a country as barren and sparsely populated as Iceland? How was it that the authorities did not know?

She had to make certain, absolutely certain she was right. She went back to the desk and pulled a thick sheaf of maps from the top drawer. These were survey maps, the most detailed cartography available up here. They depicted the land formations and water tables for several hundred square kilometers of the Reykjanes Peninsula south of Reykjavik.

She found the map she wanted, then took out a pad and

made some hasty calculations. Given the maximum diameter of a pipe, and the amount of water and steam to be moved, a pumping relay had to be located somewhere along an arc about six miles south of the city. She drew the arc on the map, then she folded it, stuffed it into her pocket, pulled her coat off the hook by the door, and left.

It was a Sunday, and the university was mostly empty, her heels echoing loudly on the tiled floor. She got as far as the parking lot at the front of the building when she realized she had left the photos on her desk. She went back, stuffed them into a large manila envelope that she threw in the bottom drawer of her desk, and locked the drawer. She took out her pad again and quickly scribbled a note to a very dear friend. She had no real reason for writing the note to him in particular . . . just something at the back of her mind told her it might be wise.

"Dear Nick," she wrote. "Have discovered something up here that is truly incredible. I'm afraid I'm about to get mixed up in some nasty local politics. Will tell you more when I see you in Washington next month. Love, Lydia."

She put the note into an envelope, addressed it to Nick Carter, care of a post office box in Washington, D.C., then put a stamp on it and stuffed it into her pocket.

The land south of Reykjavik is covered with a layer of black ash, fallout from an eruption of Mount Hekla in 1948. Not a twig or stick grows in the field, and the overall effect is a landscape as bleak and as barren as the far side of the moon. As Lydia Coatsworth's small rented car putted into this black area, leaving the city behind, she felt a sudden chill, as though she were entering the Land of the Dead. She always felt this way when she came up here. It was silly, she told herself. The sun was shining, and she'd been on this road dozens of times in her trips between the lab and the observation post at the fissure. Still, for some reason, the place gave her the creeps, especially today.

She drove slowly, examining every rock formation and dip

in the landscape as if she were seeing it for the first time. If the pumping station were out here somewhere, it was well hidden, for she'd never seen it. Never even seen anyone on this road.

No, she thought. That wasn't quite true. There was a man she encountered from time to time. He drove a rusted-out Saab, she remembered now. He was a large man. She'd waved the first time she had seen him, but he had not returned the greeting. The second time, she did not wave; in fact she barely even noticed him. A taciturn local, nothing more.

She was wondering about him when something caught her eye and made her slam down hard on the brake pedal, bringing the car to a sliding halt. A power line running parallel to the highway, which she had seen and ignored a dozen times, now seemed odd to her. Something was wrong. Suddenly she realized what had struck her as being out of place. From one of the large insulators above, a cable ran down the girder and disappeared into a conduit underground. She got out of the car and let her eyes scan the horizon. There were no houses, no buildings. No need for electricity out here.

A pump would need a source of power, she told herself. A gas generator would eat gallons of gasoline or diesel fuel, and make a lot of noise. She pulled up the collar of her coat against the chill wind and headed for a large, dark mound on the horizon in the distance. It was the only possible place something could be hidden from view of passing motorists.

It took nearly an hour to hike across the field of cinders and ash. Half the leather had been scuffed from the toes of her boots and her feet felt like lead. Twice she'd told herself she was chasing shadows. No matter what the physical evidence, a project this big was impossible to hide in Iceland.

She rounded the far side of the huge mound, and her previous qualms about the long, probably fruitless walk and the improbability of her theory suddenly evaporated. Nestled between two hills of cinder, painted black for camouflage from the air, was a hooked drainage pipe. Probably an overload unit of some sort for the pipeline that certainly was below.

Her heart leaped into her mouth. She approached the pipe very slowly, half expecting something or someone to jump out at her. She ran her hand along the smooth surface. The metal was vibrating. The pump was not far away, and it was working.

She should go back, she told herself. Get someone. Petur Tomasson. He'd know whom to contact. He could come out here with a crew.

A door slammed somewhere close, the sound very distinct out in the open. Boots crunched across the cinders. She froze next to the pipe, her pulse beating in her throat.

A car door slammed, and an engine started. In the cleavage between the two hills she caught a glimpse of a rusted-out Saab heading for the road, and then it was gone.

A flood of relief washed over her, but in the next instant she realized the man—whoever he was—would see her car parked down on the road. He'd have to wonder where she had gone.

It was terribly important for her at this moment not to be seen. She decided it would be better if she waited up there. Behind the mounds, out of sight of the road. If he came back, she could run the other way. But if he hadn't returned within fifteen minutes or so, it would probably mean he wasn't coming back. Maybe he hadn't seen her car. Maybe he hadn't even noticed it.

She brushed the ash off the pipe and leaned back against it. The wind made an odd moan as it swept unimpeded over the hills from the ocean that was not too far away. There was no movement out here. No life . . . other than the man. Even the sun seemed to stand still in the sky.

But Lydia Coatsworth was, among other things, an impatient woman when she was nervous, and she began to see the absurdity of her situation here. Damnit. She was a scientist, after all, with an international reputation. There weren't any

No Trespassing signs posted here. She was within her rights to explore the countryside off the road.

She dusted herself off and headed around the hill. She had heard a door slamming. A heavy, metal door. About fifty yards around the far edge of the hill she came upon what at first appeared to be an old-fashioned fallout shelter; a steel door was set into a steel bulwark of cinder block. In front of it a section of land had been leveled off to accommodate several vehicles.

Her mouth started to go dry again, and she began to have second thoughts about what she was doing. She didn't need this, she told herself. She was a scientist, not a private eye. A quiet life of study—wasn't that why she had gotten into this business? Nobody said anything about ferreting out energy thieves.

Still, there was the door and behind it . . . what? Proof? Summoning up her courage, she walked up and found it was unlocked. She gave a little push, and the door fell open.

Inside, it was pitch-dark. She groped along the wall for a light switch, found one, and a caged bulb flashed on overhead.

She was standing in a large, immaculately clean tiled room with a concrete floor. On the wall in front of her was a series of dials and wheel valves set into a burnished metal control panel. The constant humming told her that a gigantic engine of some sort was at work somewhere beneath her.

Two doors led off this main room. She chose the one to the left, opened it, and switched on the light. She found herself on a catwalk above two stories of pipe maze, all seemingly color-coded, gleaming as though this were a brand-new installation.

She killed the light, walked back into the control room, closed the door, and crossed to the second door. As she opened it a cloud of cement dust rose to meet her. She flipped on the switch.

The room was huge, bigger than the other two combined, and only half-finished. Scaffolding towered overhead, and the floor was strewn with construction debris and plastic drop cloths. From the size of it, it looked as though they'd hollowed out the entire inside of the mound. Whoever *they* were, they were up to something much bigger than just siphoning off a little geothermal energy.

A piece of machinery the size of a small house stood in one corner on a bed of massive timbers. She walked over and threw back a piece of the protective plastic covering. It looked familiar somehow. The tag dangling from the valve wheel was in German. It gave the port of origin as Mainz. Mainz . . . what did she know about Mainz? Then it struck her. Mainz was where Steuben and Sons had their foundry. They were the largest manufacturers of nuclear reactor components in the world. She had done a paper on the subject in her first year of graduate school. Her professor had believed that if students wanted to study geology, they might just as well understand the significance of their finds . . . such as the uses of nuclear fuels. And he never allowed any of his students to do anything by half. She had learned her subject well.

She threw back more of the cover. It was coming back to her now. All of it. This was a type of water pump that regulated the amount of coolant to a reactor's core. A nuclear reactor. What on earth would anyone want with a nuclear reactor in Iceland?

Tires crunched on the cinders outside, the sound coming in through a ventilation shaft. A car door slammed.

Quickly she tried to cover the pump, but she could not get the plastic sheet completely over the valves. She gave up and ran for the door.

She dashed through the control room, then ran down the stairway from the catwalk to the lower floor of the maze of pipes. Maybe here among the multicolored metal she would be able to conceal herself until it was safe to leave. She hadn't done anything illegal, yet she had a very odd feeling about this place. To begin with, who would run off leaving the door to a nuclear reactor building site open?

It was dark, the only illumination coming from a pair of lighted dials on a large control panel at the room's center. She threaded her way through the maze of plumbing until she reached a wall. She followed it for several feet until she found an elbow joint in a large pipe. She crawled behind it.

The door opening onto the catwalk flew open with a bang, and the light went on. To her horror, she saw a line of footprints in the dust leading from the bottom of the stairs to where she hid. She bit her tongue to keep from crying out.

He came down the stairs like a hunter stalking his prey, stopping every few feet to cock his head as if he were listening for something. She caught a glimpse of him through the tangle of pipes. He wore mechanic's overalls, and a huge black revolver rode in his right hand.

Now she'd done it, she chided herself. The scientist with the international reputation, with the right to look around if she saw something suspicious, was in a jam.

He'd found the footprints and was looking in her direction. Instinctively she cowered lower into her tiny refuge and felt her foot wedge between two pipes.

He came slowly toward where she was hiding, and their eyes met. He brought the pistol up, then came the rest of the way around the pipe.

"I guess you found me," she said, raising her hands over her head and trying to stand. But her foot was wedged solidly, and she fell forward.

He fired.

A vicious clang resounded through the room. Then a hissing sound quickly rose to a scream as white-hot steam blasted somewhere behind her. She screamed in pain as she pulled frantically at her foot, but it refused to move. The steam increased, billowing around her now, and the pain became suddenly more than she could bear, and she knew that she was going to die here, watched by the man in the mechanic's overalls.

Her back was searing . . . she was being scalded alive.

"Help me . . ." she tried to scream, but the words died in her throat. Darkness was overtaking her. It welled up from somewhere below, finally swallowing her.

ONE

As the wheels of Nick Carter's plane bumped down on the runway at Keflavik International Airport outside Reykjavik, he looked out the window at the barren, seemingly moonlike landscape and shook his head. It was nearly impossible to believe that Lydia was dead. And here, of all places.

As he made his way in line with the other passengers across the tarmac to the terminal, he got a good look at the low, featureless hills that seemed to meld into the horizon, into the low-slung, featureless sky. She had probably been happy here, with the fumaroles and lava beds and glaciers. At least she'd died working.

He collected his bag, had it checked by a perfunctory customs officer, then carried it the block or so to the airport bus terminal. The bus came promptly, a modern affair with tall, bus-tour type windows, and as he settled into his seat, the blank sky and the rocky barrenness of Iceland seemed to bear down on him. If it weren't a fit place to die, it certainly was a suitable place to mourn. The entire landscape seemed to be in mourning.

He and Lydia had been friends for several years, though it hadn't begun that way. It had started as just another conquest. A quick, easy seduction to see what came up, like a roll of the dice. It had been after a particularly difficult assignment, and he had not been himself. He had been short-tempered, cooly arrogant, and definitely, to use her words, a bastard.

She'd lain awake that night long after they'd finished, while he slept fitfully. About dawn he felt her smooth, warm body nestle against his, and he responded to her, but she held him off.

"Don't," she said.

"What's the matter?"

"Just hold me."

"I don't know you well enough for that," he had said, or something equally as lousy, and she had begun to cry. He studied her face in the early-morning light, and a rising pity for her was mixed with anger at himself for the cruelty of what he had just said and thoughts about AXE, the highly secret intelligence agency for which he worked. He was an agent. Killmaster, N3 . . . licensed to kill, just like in the James Bond novels, but for real. He also thought about the many roles he had to play, including, occasionally, that of assassin. It was the pressure, he told himself. Nothing more.

"I'm sorry," he said.

"You're a bastard."

That was that, he had thought. He had fully expected her to get up, get dressed, and leave then and there. But to his surprise her fingertips trailed softly across his shoulder blades.

"We . . . we can make love again . . . if you'd like, Nick."

When they had first met, he had seen a bored scientist who had given to him the holier-than-thou routine. She was above him, but she might consent to perhaps make love. She was slumming. But now he knew he had been mistaken. As he looked into her eyes, he saw something else, something much more honest and infinitely more dangerous.

"I love your body," she murmured softly, running her hand down his collarbone and across the stiff, hard shell of the scar from an old bullet wound.

He kissed her then, long and full, and for the first time

something buried deep inside her came to life, and she clung
to him as if she never wanted to let him go.

"Oh . . . God," she moaned, her fingernails digging into
his back.

"It's all right, Lydia," Carter whispered, and after a long
time she began to relax, and she laid back, her eyes moist.

He kissed her breasts, then, the nipples erect, and worked
his way slowly down to her flat stomach, and the small tuft of
pubic hair as she spread her legs for him.

"Nick," she whimpered, holding his head between her
hands, her hips gyrating.

He rose up, kissing her breasts as he entered her, and soon
they were making slow, gentle love, her body coming up to
meet his thrusts. And it was good. Much better than it had
been for Carter for a very long time.

After that night and morning together they had gone their
separate ways: he to Peru to take care of a Communist
guerrilla defection the CIA was on the verge of mishandling;
and she to the mountains of Montana to study igneous rock
formations. But she had written from time to time. Timidly at
first, a line or two, just to let him know she was alive and
well, then longer letters, more of herself, but always careful
never to infringe on him . . . never to ask questions.

They met again in Washington. He was on leave between
assignments, and she had returned to write a grant for George
Washington University. They dined in Georgetown, attended a concert at the Kennedy Center, then checked into the
Watergate for a night of champagne and lovemaking that
culminated at the rooftop pool at about five that morning.

It was while sitting there, dangling his feet in the tepid
water, watching her absolutely perfect form break the surface
then dip again beneath the moon-jeweled wavelets, that he
wondered if AXE could do without him for a few years, and if
he could do without AXE.

But it wasn't to be. The phone rang the next morning and
he'd picked it up, feeling better and more relaxed than he had
in years. It was David Hawk, AXE's two-fisted director,

with the usual summons. This time to Lahore, where supply lines for the Afghan nationalists were in serious danger of being cut off. They said their good-byes again. She said she understood, although he suspected she didn't. And shortly after that she had accepted the faculty job with the University of Iceland for a year. It was a chance to study the fissures she had talked about. It was to be the last time they would ever see one another.

A month later he'd come back to Washington, the supply lines flowing once again, to be greeted by a very odd piece of mail. A large brown envelope postmarked Iceland with a Thorstein Josepsson, Althing Committee on Internal Affairs, on the return address. Inside was another envelope, this one badly water-damaged, and a letter. The letter spoke in somber tones of regrets and condolences, and told of a freak accident in a geyser field, a foot caught, and a horrible scalding death. She'd been carrying a letter, sealed, stamped but never sent.

Lydia's letter was incendiary. His suspicions burned. What had she found? How did it figure in the local politics? What *were* the local politics?

He had appealed to Hawk for a week's leave and was offered three days. But Hawk saw the look in his eyes and gave him a no-limit on the time as long as he was willing to be on twenty-four-hour call. He'd agreed, got cash and a ticket on his credit card, and boarded the first flight to Iceland. Now that he was here, however, in full view of the melancholy sky and the tired sea pounding its worn waves time after time against the shore, he wondered if he hadn't made a mistake. After all, there was absolutely no reason to suspect she hadn't died exactly as Josepsson had written. Maybe he should have gone to the Caribbean or to the Mediterranean, someplace light and airy where the atmosphere wouldn't contribute to his gloom. He was full of sadness and regrets.

The bus pulled into Austurvollur Square and stopped in front of a building that advertised itself as the Borg Hotel. "Final stop," the driver said through the public-address system. Other buses were lined up outside.

Carter followed the crowd to the front of the bus, then leaned over the driver's seat.

The man looked up at him.

"Tell me about the Althing."

"It's our Parliament. Oldest continuously meeting parliament in the world. Dates back to 930 A.D. Meets over there." The driver indicated a nineteenth-century two-story stone building on the other side of the square.

"Is it in session now?"

"No," the driver said. "It is summer vacation."

"They're all gone then?" Carter asked, looking at the building.

"Some of them remain here. There are offices. There is work to be done."

He thanked the man and got out. A few minutes later he picked his bag up from the sidewalk where the driver had pitched it, then went inside the hotel. They had a room, but it was small and had no view of the harbor. He took it. A bellman carried his suitcase upstairs, and when the young man was finished opening the drapes and closet doors and explaining hotel policy, Carter gave him a folded bill.

"Have you ever heard of Thorstein Josepsson?" he asked.

The bellman looked at the money, then up at Carter. He nodded. "He's a distinguished member of the Althing."

"Where does he live?"

"Here, in town."

"What else do you know about him?"

The bellman hesitated. Carter peeled off another bill and handed it over.

"He likes scotch whiskey, no ice, no water. Usually eats his dinner here in the hotel dining room."

Carter smiled. "What else does he do?"

"Mr. Josepsson is on the board of directors of the Icelandic Internal Energy Commission, and is on the boards of several large businesses."

"Where can I find him?"

"At this moment, sir?"

Carter nodded.

"I believe Mr. Josepsson is downstairs in the dining room."

Carter handed the bellman another bill. "Meet me downstairs in five minutes, and point him out to me."

"Very good, sir."

When the bellman was gone, Carter locked the door and began unpacking with his customary caution. He pulled all the drapes, and when the room was quite dark, he turned on the lights. He checked the walls, outlets, and fixtures for signs of anything unusual. Even though no one knew he was coming up here, this was standard operating procedure. When he found nothing, he put his suitcase on the bed and unlocked it.

From an inside pocket he took out a shoulder holster, the leather of which had been worn dark with use, and he strapped it on. Then he pulled out a radio-cassette player, removed the back, then the main component board. Inside, in a Styrofoam mold, lay Wilhelmina, his 9mm Luger, and below it a silencer. The player had been made by AXE technicians to allow Carter to carry his weapons aboard commercial flights without detection. He pocketed the silencer, then took out the gun and pushed it into the holster.

From inside the suitcase's satin lining he drew out a narrow sheath of chamois leather and a pencil-thin blade with a wickedly sharp point. He strapped the sheath to his forearm under his shirt and inserted the stiletto, years ago nicknamed Hugo. Then he buttoned the shirt over it and put on his jacket. He studied his image in the full-length mirror on the back of the bathroom door. When he was satisfied that none of his weaponry showed, he closed the suitcase and shoved it under the bed, then left, locking the door behind him.

He carried another weapon as well, a gas bomb dubbed Pierre, attached to his leg, high on his right thigh, much like a third testicle. Any other man thus loaded down would have felt like a walking arsenal, but Carter had been dressing this way for a good many years and had had occasion to call on each of his weapons in time of crisis. Consequently, for the first time since leaving Washington, he felt fully secure and ready for anything.

The bellman stepped up to him as he entered the dining room and handed him a folded white card. Carter opened it and found a schematic drawing of the dining room, showing three tables in front of a bay of large windows at the far end of the room. At one of the tables the bellman had made a check mark.

Carter glanced across the room. The man sitting at that position was neither old nor young, but like many Icelanders Carter had seen, he had rugged, rocklike features that seemed to have been borrowed from the landscape. Two other men were seated with him, and they looked decidedly foreign . . . that is, foreign to Iceland.

Carter reached into his pocket for an additional tip, but the bellman, apparently not interested in being involved any further with the American and his questions, had moved away. Carter shrugged, then went across the room to where Josepsson was seated.

"Mr. Josepsson," Carter said.

The man looked up inquiringly, a bite of fish still in his mouth.

"I am Nick Carter. The addressee of the letter from Dr. Lydia Coatsworth you were kind enough to forward to me."

The man put down his knife and fork, laid his napkin on the table, and rose to shake Carter's hand. "We were terribly saddened, Mr. Carter. You were a close friend of Dr. Coatsworth?"

"Yes, I was."

"I am sorry, truly sorry then."

There was an awkward moment where signals seemed to have gotten crossed, then Carter gave a slight nod, acknowledging the man's expression of sympathy.

"Do you mind if I sit down?" It was pushing things, but Carter wanted to see how Josepsson would react.

Josepsson glanced uncertainly at the other two men who watched from across the table. Carter's request to join them clearly made him uncomfortable, but he had no polite way of refusing.

"Please do," he said at last. "We have an empty place."

Carter drew up a chair, and Josepsson motioned for the waiter.

Carter scanned the menu, and when the waiter arrived, he started to order, but Josepsson cut him off. "Your first visit to our country?" he asked.

Carter nodded.

"Then have the fish. Any fish. It is always best in Iceland."

Carter pointed to an entree with an unpronounceable Icelandic name. The waiter nodded, wrote it down, then gathered up the menu and left.

"May I introduce Herr Hofstaeder and Herr Boorman. Some business associates of mine."

Carter nodded to the two men, and they returned the perfunctory greeting. Hofstaeder looked every inch the typical German in his middle sixties, light-skinned, brown hair light enough to blend in with the gray and make it difficult at first glance to tell his age. His friend, Boorman, however, was another matter. Younger—in his late thirties—his hair was jet black and his skin olive-toned. Streaks of gray had just begun to appear at the temples, giving him a dashing, somewhat Latin look.

"What brings you to Iceland, Mr. Carter?" Josepsson asked without preamble. "I imagine you will want to see the university where Dr. Coatsworth worked, and perhaps travel to the interior to see the accident site. I'm guessing now as to why you have chosen this moment to visit us."

"Did you read her letter?" Carter asked, keeping his voice neutral.

"No. It was sealed. We merely sent it to whom it was addressed. It was a simple administrative matter. You must understand, Mr. Carter, that I did not know Dr. Coatsworth personally."

"She indicated to me, Mr. Josepsson, that she had found something here. Something incredible, she wrote, that would stir up the local politics. Would you have any idea what she could have meant by that?"

For the second time Josepsson looked obviously uncomfortable. He glanced at the other two men, then glanced at his fingernails. "No," he said finally. "I have no idea. You should, perhaps, go to the university. Perhaps they can be of more help."

"I will. But I wanted to make contact with you first, sir. You did send me her letter."

"It is a mystery to me what she may have meant," Josepsson said. He took a drink of water. "But I was the sponsor for the exchange program that brought Dr. Coatsworth to our country. I saw it as my logical duty to forward her letter to you, as well as her personal effects to her family. You must understand."

Carter said nothing; he was thinking again of the last time they had been together.

"I have no knowledge of what she may have discovered that could have had any effect on our politics . . . though I feel I speak with some authority when I say I cannot imagine what she might have been referring to." Josepsson leaned forward slightly. "You must understand, Mr. Carter, that here in Iceland politics are a good deal more honest and aboveboard than they are anywhere else in the world. The United States included." He dabbed his napkin on his lips and laid it on his plate. "Now, if you will excuse us, Mr. Carter, we still have a great deal of business to attend to. You must understand."

Josepsson and the other two got to their feet.

Carter stood up and shook their hands. "It's quite all right," he said. "Thank you for your assistance."

"Good day, sir," Josepsson said. The other two bowed, then they all left.

Carter watched them leave, then he made a soft, low whistle under his breath. He'd wanted to see Josepsson's reaction when he mentioned the contents of Lydia's letter, and he guessed he'd seen it, although he hadn't expected the man's behavior to be so obvious. There was a lot the man wasn't saying . . . and a lot he was hiding. What?

In a few minutes the waiter showed up with a platter of marinated herring and a half-dozen pieces of pumpernickel bread. Carter made a quick meal of it, then paid his bill and caught a cab in front of the hotel. He instructed the driver to take him to the University of Iceland campus.

It had occurred to him that since Iceland derived all of its energy from geothermal sources, the Icelandic Internal Energy Commission's responsibilities concerned the steam wells located in the lava beds, and now, as the chimneyless buildings of Reykjavik rushed toward him through the speeding cab's windows, he wondered if there wasn't some connection between Thorstein Josepsson, Iceland's Internal Energy Commission, and whatever project Lydia had been working on when she died.

The university campus consisted of four monolithic buildings set into a barren, rock-strewn field on the south side of the city. The cab pulled up in front of the largest of these, and Carter paid the driver and headed up the sidewalk toward the main entrance. A young student with long blond hair was just coming out of the building, and he stopped her to ask where he might find the geology department. She smiled enchantingly and motioned toward the second building down, which she said housed all the natural sciences.

He thanked her, marveling at the ease with which everyone here spoke English. Icelandic is basically Old Norse, which the Vikings spoke in the tenth century. It is a complicated, highly inflected language with several consonants foreign to English. Although Carter spoke a little Danish, and understood both Swedish and Norwegian, he was thankful he did not have to converse with people here in their native tongue.

The door to the geology department's administrative office was one of a series along a narrow corridor. Carter was about to open it and go in when something on the wall outside caught his eye. Pinned to a bulletin board, framed in black, was a photo of Lydia. Although it wasn't exactly as he remembered her, he figured it must have been the snapshot she submitted with her application. Probably an old school picture. He'd known a mature woman, eyes full of knowledge of the world . . . frank yet bittersweet, the corners of her mouth slightly lined. And yet here was the photograph of a young woman . . . cheeks blooming, a gleaming smile, eyes bright and full of promise. She looked very innocent and very beautiful. It was hard to believe that she was dead.

"Pity, isn't it?" asked a lanky, red-haired man who had stopped to study Carter while Carter studied the photograph.

Carter looked at him.

"Did you know her?"

"Yes, I did."

"In America?"

"Yes, there," Carter said. "You worked with her here?"

"We were colleagues. I am Dr. Petur Tomasson. You?" he said, extending his hand.

Carter shook it. "Nick Carter. I think you're the man I came here to speak with."

"I beg your pardon?"

"Lydia wrote me of you. And of her work. I'd like to know more about both. Is there someplace we can talk?"

Tomasson looked at him for a long moment, then nodded. "This way," he said. He went down the corridor, around a corner, and through a steel door with a thick quartz window set into it at eye level. "The lab," Tomasson said tersely. "My office is in the rear."

They went through the lab, which was filled with a variety of modern, up-to-date, and very expensive equipment, while Carter explained about Lydia's letter.

"And now you've come to me to see if I know what it is she found, is that it?" asked Tomasson.

They came into his tiny cubicle of an office, which was nothing more than a tiny room, filled with books and journals, containing a worktable and two chairs.

Tomasson went behind the table and sat down, motioning

for Carter to take the other chair.

"She seemed concerned, and now she's dead," Carter said, sitting down. "I'd like to know what she was working on."

Tomasson shrugged. "But I have no idea. None whatsoever. Several days before her accident, we talked about a project I've been working on, which is not at all related to what happened, I'm sure. I needed her input on some ideas I'd come up with, and she gave her ideas as freely as she always did. But I'm sure if she'd found anything 'incredible,' as she reported to you in her letter, she would have said something. We had no secrets from one another, professionally, that is."

"Maybe she thought what she found was potentially dangerous. Maybe she thought she was protecting you by not saying anything."

"Perhaps," said Tomasson, touching a match to the tobacco in his pipe.

"Just what was she working on?"

"There has been some new volcanic activity a bit offshore of the Reykjanes Peninsula. Not far from here, actually. That sort of thing was right down her alley."

"But she was in the interior when she died. Miles from the ocean."

"That's true. I have no idea what she could have been doing there."

"Would it be possible to see where she was . . . where she died?"

Tomasson had picked up the hesitation. "You don't think it was an accident, do you."

"I don't know. Can I get to the site?"

The man was silent for a long moment. "Yes, it's possible to go there. One has to have a Land-Rover—and some equipment, of course. She died in a rather inaccessible place. It would also help to have someone along who knew the area."

Carter played with a pencil for a moment, thinking. "Did Lydia have an office here?"

"Yes, she did, as did all of the staff. But I believe we sent her personal effects to her family in Ohio."

"What about her notes, her scientific data, that sort of thing?"

"It all belongs to the university, Mr. Carter."

"I understand that. Is it still here?"

"Yes. It's still in her office."

"May I see it?"

Tomasson got to his feet and opened the door of his office. "I have a feeling if I said no, you'd see it anyway." He beckoned to Carter, and they walked across the lab. Several students had shown up to use the small seismographic laboratory and developing room to one side of the lab, and they all looked up with curiosity. Tomasson ignored them, puffing on his pipe in a preoccupied way. The revelation of Lydia's letter seemed to have disturbed him.

Lydia's office was only slightly smaller than Tomasson's and differed in layout only in that it had a window that looked out across the parking lot, and to the ocean beyond.

"There's nothing here," Carter said. The shelves were bare, and the desk had been stripped of everything except a lamp.

"Most of it was either sent to her relatives or returned to university stock. Reference books, tools, that sort of thing."

Carter pulled out several of the desk drawers, which were mostly empty. The large bottom drawer, however, was locked. "What about this one?"

Tomasson came around the desk. "I forgot all about it. It's locked. I was hoping the key would turn up. But I got busy and it slipped my mind."

Carter took a thin metal pick from the seam of his wallet and inserted it into the lock. In a few moments it popped open.

Tomasson said nothing, but his lips were compressed.

Carter poured the contents of the drawer onto the desk top and rummaged through the files and papers until he found a sealed manila envelope with photos inside. He pushed the rest of the papers to one side to make room for them.

"What's this?" Tomasson asked, his professional curiosity piqued.

"Your guess is as good as mine," Carter said. "Any ideas?"

"It's some kind of a time sequence," Tomasson said, studying the photos. "The times are stamped." He shuffled through the photos, laying them in order.

Carter noticed the date stamped on the shots. It was the day before she died.

"This was probably the fissure she was studying. She did mention something about it."

"These were taken the day before she died. One day at the seashore. The next inland. Isn't that odd?"

Tomasson shook his head. "I don't know. But I would not go looking for deep dark plots, Mr. Carter. We are scientists here, not spies."

"Still, it's odd."

"Yes," Tomasson admitted. He was staring at the photos.

"Do these photos mean anything to you? Do they fit in with what it was she was working on?"

"I don't know. It'll take some analyzing."

"Will you do it?"

"Yes. It may take a few hours. Maybe a day."

"I'll be back tomorrow. I'm going to rent myself a Land-Rover and a guide."

Tomasson looked up. "Let me give you a word of advice, Mr. Carter. Sometimes strange things happen here. I don't want to unduly alarm you, but I do want you to be careful."

"Thank you."

Tomasson nodded, then started gathering up the photos.

Carter telephoned for a cab from the lobby of the university's main building, and while he waited for it to come he did some thinking. He was certain now that Lydia had not met with any accident, although he did not really know what made him so sure. It was just a very strong hunch.

He was also reasonably sure that Josepsson had something to do with whatever political trouble Lydia had mentioned.

The man was hiding something, definitely hiding something, and it was time, Carter thought, to begin drawing the man out.

The cab came, and as they started down the highway that led into Reykjavik, a small, black Lancia pulled out behind them.

TWO

When they arrived at the Borg Hotel, Carter got out and was paying the driver when he noticed the Lancia parked just down the street. He went upstairs to his room.

As he opened the door he saw a small piece of notepaper he'd stuck in the doorjamb. It had fallen out. Someone had been in the room since he had left.

The place looked untouched, but he took out his gun and carefully checked the bathroom and closet. No one was there. From beneath his bed he pulled out his suitcase. Both locks had been forced, and every piece of clothing had been shredded. The lining of the suitcase had been ripped out all the way to the leather.

This had been no casual search. This was harassment, pure and simple, and whoever had done it felt no need to be subtle.

He went to the telephone and dialed for the operator. "Desk," said a mellow female voice.

"This is Carter in six-oh-eight. Someone's been in my room, and whoever it was used a master key. There's no sign the lock has been tampered with."

"Sir, the maid service enters each room about midday."

"Since when does the maid service shred clothing and destroy suitcases? Please send up your security people."

"Yes, sir. Right away, sir."

He slammed the phone down. He could ignore this, he

29

thought. Obviously this tactic was intended to frighten him, but whoever was responsible didn't know Carter. Letting it slide wouldn't be in keeping with his cover as an average citizen. Besides, the use of the master key implied the hotel had allowed it to happen, and he wanted to see what would come of raising a little hell with the management.

While he waited for the hotel to react, he called the coroner's office. A pleasant-sounding young woman told him in perfect English that any information he might require concerning the location of Lydia Coatsworth's accident would have to be obtained from the local authorities—in this case the police of Akureyri, the major town of Northern Iceland, about an hour from Reykjavik by air.

He hung up and placed a second call to the travel agency office in the hotel lobby. He made a reservation on a domestic Icelandic Airlines flight to Akureyri at 3:00 that afternoon and arranged to have a Land-Rover from one of the local outing clubs waiting for him when he arrived.

As he hung up from talking to the travel agency, a brisk knock sounded at the door. He opened it to find two men standing in the corridor. One was large, grim, and had a handshake like a vise. He introduced himself as the house detective. The other was smaller, more nervous, and his hands were noticeably damp. His name, he said, was Magnus Thoroddson. He was the assistant manager.

"Come in, gentlemen," said Carter. "I'd like to show you something." He motioned them over to the suitcase that lay open on the bed. "I returned from a business meeting a few moments ago, and this is what I came back to."

The detective lifted out a sport shirt that had been slashed. "I didn't see any evidence that the door had been forced," the man said. "Did you lend your key to someone?"

"Of course not," Carter snapped petulantly. "In point of fact, obviously a master key was used." He said this looking directly at the assistant manager.

Thoroddson looked away, frowning. He gingerly picked

out a pair of designer jeans that looked as though they'd been caught in a lawnmower. "Why are you in Iceland, Mr. Carter?" he asked pointedly.

"I'm investigating the death of a friend."

"I see. Apparently someone doesn't want you to investigate it."

"That thought crossed my mind," said Carter.

"Then it is a private matter between you and the party, whoever it is, who doesn't want you here. It has nothing to do with the hotel."

"A master key was used. Surely this indicates some negligence on the part of your hotel."

"We have many master keys. Every maid carries one," the house detective said.

"Let's discuss it with your staff, in that case," Carter said, raising his voice.

"There is no need to become angry, Mr. Carter," Thoroddson said hastily. "The hotel will make full restitution, of course, provided that you find other accommodations within twenty-four hours."

"No need for that," Carter said stiffly. "I've decided to leave in any event."

"I see," said Thoroddson. "In that case there will be no bill, of course. Within an hour there will be a check for you at the desk to cover the damages. I'm terribly sorry this happened."

"Why haven't you called the police?" Carter asked. "It seems obvious that a crime has been committed."

Thoroddson cast an uncomfortable glance at the detective. "That's certainly an option," he said. "If you wish to call them, by all means . . ."

"I have a feeling I wouldn't get much satisfaction from them, either. Thank you for your time. I'll pack what few intact belongings I have left and check out immediately."

The two men turned and went to the door.

"You can tell Josepsson that it's going to take a lot more

than ruining my wardrobe to frighten me out of Iceland,"
Carter said.

"I . . . I beg your pardon?" said the assistant manager,
turning back.

"Just pass along the message," Carter said. When they
were gone he closed and locked his door.

He grabbed his coat, stuffed his mutilated clothing back
into the suitcase, and fastened it as best he could. He left the
hotel by the rear exit, throwing his suitcase into a trash bin in
the alley.

When he reached the sidewalk, the black Lancia was idling
at the curb, the driver casually reading a newspaper. He came
up to the driver's window and tapped. The man rolled it
down, his eyes round. Carter stuck the Luger in his face.

"Tell your boss to back off," he said. "I'll find out what
happened to Lydia Coatsworth . . . you can assure him of
that."

The man swallowed hard but said nothing.

"And stop following me."

The driver nodded but held his silence.

Carter holstered his gun and headed away. The Lancia
remained where it was parked.

He started walking and found a small sporting goods store
on a back street half a mile away. Inside he told the clerk that
he was planning a trip to see the glaciers in the center of the
island and needed a complete outfitting. It had been a slow
day, and the clerk gave him his undivided attention. Within a
short time, Carter had purchased a sleeping bag, a wardrobe
of heavy clothing, hiking boots, a compass, line and other
things, including packs to carry the gear.

He took a cab out to the airport, and a couple of hours later
he was looking down from ten thousand feet on a delta of dry
creeks and branches that extended over the landscape like
nerve endings. Then the wing flaps ground down, and the
plane began its descent into Akureyri.

He had left a clear trail, he thought. Any amateur would

know where he was going. He only hoped that he'd made himself appear dangerous enough to whoever was behind all this to warrant the effort of being killed.

He didn't know for certain that it had been Josepsson, although he felt from their conversation in the restaurant that the man was implicated in some way. But whoever it was would have to tip his hand when he sent in the assassin.

They landed, and Carter picked up the Land-Rover. He drove directly to the local police headquarters, where the officer at the front desk greeted him pleasantly enough until he gathered that Carter had come to turn what had already been declared an accident into a possible murder case, at which time his demeanor cooled noticeably, and Carter was referred brusquely to a Captain Einar Einarsson.

The captain, a tall, husky man, was busy in a back room when Carter came in. He looked up and listened to Carter's request, then turned from his typing with a patient sigh and asked Carter to have a seat.

"Mr. Carter, your story and suspicions are interesting, but Dr. Coatsworth was not murdered near Reykjavik and her body transported to Akureyri as you suggest. I was the officer in charge of the investigation, and I can say with certainty that is not the way it happened."

"I see," Carter said. Instinctively he liked the man.

"Dr. Coatsworth died at the foot of Mount Askja, some one hundred kilometers from here. The time of her death and the time of the discovery of her body were much too close together to allow her to have been taken from one place to another."

"Unless she had been packed in ice, perhaps, her body cooled before it was transported," Carter suggested.

"Highly unlikely. Besides, it seems like a lot of trouble to disguise a murder scene."

"What about the people who discovered her? Can their stories be believed?"

"Members of the local outing club. All of them friends of

mine. Known them all my life. They are telling the truth.''

"I'd still like to look into it myself.''

"I don't have the manpower . . .''

"If you could just show me where her body was found. Perhaps you have a map? It would be a great help.''

Einarsson shook his head. "I do not know who you are, Mr. Carter, but very well.'' He got up and produced a map from a file cabinet. He brought it back to his desk. Carter got to his feet.

"Here,'' the captain said, pointing to a spot inland. "Her body was just here.'' He marked the spot with a penciled cross.

"Thank you,'' Carter said. "I appreciate your help.''

But the captain had sat back down and had already gone back to his typing.

That evening Carter downed a heavy meal at the local hotel, then climbed into the Land-Rover and headed south, out of town, the car's big wheels pounding over the ruts on the dirt track.

He rounded the end of Eyjafjördur, the narrow inlet that formed Akureyri's waterway to the sea, then turned southeast toward the fireball sun into some of the most desolate, God-forsaken country he had ever seen.

Akureyri was within sixty miles of the Arctic Circle. No grass grew here away from the sea; there was only rock from one horizon to the other. Along the coasts there was occa-sional rain. Back here it hardly ever rained, and only a small amount of snow blew down from the mountains.

From the air, he'd thought the place looked stripped, desolate, a far outpost for the machinations of man. Once he'd landed and gotten some perspective on its true size, he thought the place seemed unreal . . . like a stage set for a play. But now, as the last view of Akureyri faded into the distance, and he confronted the land as a lone individual, he began to realize the true immensity of it.

In the far distance against the thin gray line of the horizon, a mountain lay like a deflated black bag, its top shorn off. Valleys dipped, hills rose, distinguishable only in shades of black, gray, and brown. There were no colors here, nothing but bland geometric land forms that seemed to stretch on forever.

Here was nature unadorned, he thought: denuded, like a woman without makeup. At first it was stunning, but then it was monotonous.

He drove for several hours but made only meager progress. The map was not very clear, and often the road got lost in dried creek beds, was blocked by fallen rock, or just petered out in a drift of pumice stone.

This had happened for the second time, and for the second time he had stopped, turned off the engine, and gotten out to kick through the bits of shale and lava rock, when his ears picked up an odd sound the wind brought from the north.

He turned and saw a speck on the horizon. He would have thought it was a bird or a gull except for the unmistakable chop of helicopter blades.

He scrambled back to the Land-Rover and gunned the engine to life. He made a wide loop until he came in contact with the road again, then pressed down on the accelerator. There was no time to lose. If they decided to fight it out with him, here in the open, he'd be a sitting duck. They could strafe him from the sky, and he'd have no place to duck.

The Land-Rover's heavy-duty springs bottomed out on the deep ruts, making it very difficult to drive. A rooster tail of dust fanned out behind him that was no doubt visible for miles, but it didn't matter. They'd seen him long before he had spotted them.

He kept his eye on the approaching machine. He hadn't counted on this. For some reason he'd envisioned this fight on the ground. He hadn't realized the landscape was so wide open, affording him so little cover. . . . Goddamnit, he was slipping. Preparation. Wasn't that the unbending rule at

Mesa Verde where AXE agents were trained? Now it looked as though he was going to have to pay for his lack of foresight.

He bounced up over a mound. Mount Askja was in the distance, stark, ancient, without a blade of grass to grace her flanks. He drove for the mountain, hoping there'd be someplace, anyplace for cover.

He pressed down even harder on the accelerator, speeding around a long, rock-strewn curve along the edge of a narrow ravine, wondering if the Land-Rover's tires would hold up much longer, when he spotted what appeared to be a building. It was almost midnight now, but the sun still lingered on the horizon. At these latitudes in midsummer it never went down. Shadows were long in the twilight, however, and the play of light and dark across the rocks easily tricked the eye, and yet, half a mile ahead on the right side of the road, a triangular shape jutted out of the landscape.

As he drew closer he could see that it was an A-frame cabin of some sort. The roof had been covered with rocks and ash to protect it from the elements, but the front wall had windows and a door. Behind him the chopper had made an abrupt about-face and was bearing down on him. It was still a long way off, but it was closing the gap very fast.

The house looked like the only hope on the barren landscape. He crunched to a halt in front of the place, grabbed his pack, and scrambled down the side of the road. The chopper's blades beat the air not far away. He glanced over his shoulder. It was heading directly up the valley, nose down, making the best time it could.

He raced for the front door on the tiny porch but stopped short at the top step. He looked back. The helicopter had slowed down. This was all wrong. Alarm bells were jangling along his nerves.

The house was the obvious place out here for him to run to. It was too neat, too convenient. He was getting the definite feeling that he had been herded to this place.

The chopper was only a few hundred yards out. The

popcorn sound of rapid fire filled the air, and dust began to kick up behind him.

They weren't aiming right. They wanted him inside.

He stepped back off the porch, tossed his pack at the door, and dove to the left. A horrendous roar hammered his eardrums, and the ground bucked beneath him as the door burst outward in a tremendous blast of flame. A huge cloud of smoke erupted from the opening as dust and debris fell like rain.

He scrambled back through the dense smoke and threw himself down at an odd angle in front of the door. Then he used a trick he'd learned on assignment in the Orient to twist his head into such a position that even the close observer would be convinced his neck was broken.

The only way to get them out of the sky, he told himself, was to convince them that their little trick had worked.

Dust scattered in the rotor wash as the helicopter set down a minute or two later. Carter had his Luger out of his holster, hidden at his side.

Someone came toward him, then stopped. His ears were still ringing from the blast. The toe of a boot jabbed him roughly in the side. He rolled over limply, being careful not to expose Wilhelmina.

The man wasn't sure. He hesitated, then bent down and pried Carter's eyelids apart. The man's expression was grim, businesslike, the look of a pro.

The realization that Carter was still alive hit him at the same moment the bullet from the Luger penetrated his heart.

His lips parted slightly, the eyes widened with surprise, and he looked as if he wanted to say something. He fell forward on top of Carter.

"Victor? Victor?" someone called anxiously from the helicopter.

Carter threw the body off at the same time the helicopter came to life and started to lift off. He got up on one knee and began firing, but the machine was gathering altitude and speed.

Carter kept on firing until the chopper was obviously out of range, then he went back to examine the man he had killed.

There was no identification on the body. The labels had been ripped out of his clothing. In his hand was a Luger much like Carter's, although from the look of it, it had probably been manufactured during the Second World War.

"Come on, Victor," Carter muttered as he holstered his Luger, lifted the body onto his shoulder, and carried it up to the Land-Rover. Victor had been a big man, well over two hundred pounds, and by the time Carter got him situated and the tailgate closed, he was breathing hard from the effort.

He trudged back to the front and looked up toward where the helicopter had disappeared. They wanted him dead pretty badly to stage something like this. It told him that indeed he was on to something.

"Is this our killer?" asked Captain Einarsson, blinking at the body in the back of the Land-Rover. Carter got the policeman's home address, called him, and then had gone out there. It was just four in the morning.

"I don't know if he killed Dr. Coatsworth," said Carter, "but he definitely tried to kill me a few hours ago."

"Never seen him before," said the captain, shaking his head. Einarsson had called for some police assistance after hearing from Carter, and he nodded to two sleepy officers standing nearby who pulled the body out of the back. "Of course, I don't know you either." He held out his hand. Carter handed over his Luger. "Let's go inside," Einarsson said.

They went into the man's tiny study at the back of the house, and Carter sat down in a small wooden chair as the captain set up a tape recorder. He laid Carter's gun on the desk, then flipped on the machine.

Without prompting, Carter told the story, leaving out only his true identity as an AXE agent. He pulled out his Amalgamated Press and Wire Service credentials and laid them on the desk along with his permit to carry the weapon.

When he finished, Einarsson flipped off the tape recorder, sat back, and looked at Carter.

"Just who are you?" he asked.

"I've already told you that, Captain. I'm a stringer with Amalgamated Press. You have my identification in front of you."

"I don't buy it."

"Call my office in Washington, D.C. My identity will be verified."

"I'm sure it would be. Which doesn't mean a damned thing."

"Do you have any reason to believe I'm not telling the truth?"

"Several reasons, as a matter of fact. Most reporters I've heard of don't go around with German Lugers under their coats. And most, although quite smart, wouldn't know a trap until it was far too late."

"Maybe I got lucky."

"Maybe." Einarsson's fingers pensively curled the corners of two sheets of paper in front of him. He seemed to be waiting for something.

Someone knocked on the door a few seconds later. Einarsson excused himself, got up, and left the room. He was gone for several minutes, during which time Carter gathered up his identification and Luger and pocketed them. When Einarsson returned, he perched on the edge of his desk. He did not seem very happy.

"That was the coroner. He's checked out this man you called Victor."

"And?"

"It's just a preliminary report. Confirms part of your story . . . that he was shot to death at close range. But Victor was a curious man."

Carter said nothing.

"The man's fingerprints were missing. They had been surgically removed. Some years ago, the doctor suggests."

The man *was* a pro, Carter thought.

"In the flesh of his underarm there was a small, surgically implanted pouch. It contained a capsule of cyanide. A thumbnail could have broken it, and the man would have died instantly. Your Victor was evidently a fanatic. No one has cyanide capsules surgically implanted for the hell of it. Now I'm going to ask you again, just who the hell are you?"

"I can't answer that, Captain. Let me just say that I'm here in Iceland as a private citizen, looking into the death of a very close friend. Believe me, I'm just as surprised about this as you are."

"Not good enough, Carter. There's been a murder in my jurisdiction. We don't get many crimes of that seriousness up here. Once every ten years or so one of the local fishermen gets drunk and kills his wife's lover. Open and shut. But I can't hide something like this in a file like they would in a big city. My ass is on the line here. People are going to ask questions."

Carter sighed. "I'll make a deal with you," he said. "I'm going to need some room to maneuver, and I'm going to need some friends in high places. If you give me the leeway and work with me on this, I promise you that you will be the first to know anything I know. You may not be able to put it in your files, but at least you'll know."

Einarsson picked up a pencil and tapped it on the desk. "That's the best I'm going to get, isn't it?"

Carter nodded. "I'm afraid so. You could have me arrested . . ."

"And you'd stay in jail until you rotted without saying a word. Provided you weren't released on orders from higher up."

Carter shrugged.

Einarsson sighed deeply. "I'm not going to try to hold you. I don't think it'd do me any good. But I will hold you to your promise. Not much happens up here, but I can make a lot of waves down in Reykjavik if need be."

Carter got up. "Thanks. I won't forget my promise."

Einarsson smiled. ''If anyone ever murders me, I'd like to think that someone like you would be on the case.''

Carter smiled, and left.

THREE

Carter drove through the clean, broad streets of Akureyri until he found a pleasant-looking hotel by the waterfront. He had a multitude of things on his mind, each one of them an unanswered question. He had not slept in almost twenty-four hours, and it was becoming increasingly difficult to think straight.

He checked in and went up to his room, leaving strict instructions with the desk clerk that he was not to be disturbed. Once upstairs, he locked the door, fell onto the bed fully clothed, and slept. It was shortly after five in the morning.

When he awoke, he called the desk and had some coffee sent up. It was just 9:30 A.M., and although he had slept only a little more than four hours, he felt somewhat refreshed.

He got the operator and had her place a long-distance call. Petur Tomasson was in his office. He answered on the second ring.

"This is Carter. Have you found anything?"

"I've been trying to get in contact with you," Tomasson shouted excitedly. "I've found something, I think, in Dr. Coatsworth's photographs."

"Just a rock formation, wasn't it?"

"That's what I thought at first, but I kept thinking about

it. I had a feeling, don't you see, that I was missing some-thing. And then I had it. The water . . ."

"What about the water?"

"She was timing the water's movement. Its vertical rise and fall against the rocks."

"The tide—" Carter started, but Tomasson interrupted him impatiently.

"No . . . no, not the tide. Something else. An upwelling of sorts. She was timing the upwellings."

"I still don't understand," Carter said, frustrated. "I'm not a geologist."

"I'll try to put it as simply as I can. Dr. Coatsworth was evidently studying some kind of an underwater eruption. She found . . . I think . . . that the phenomenon was not natural. It was man-made."

"What do you think is going on—if it's not volcanic?"

Tomasson hesitated for a moment as if he were having trouble getting the words just right. "Someone wants to disguise the fact that geothermal power is being siphoned from the hot springs outside of Reykjavik."

"Can you explain that a little more?"

"Well, beneath Iceland, there is what we call the geothermal-aquifer-interface. The lower volcanic action heats up the mid-level water layers, which in turn erupts on the surface as usable steam. And someone is tapping into it."

Carter whistled into the phone. "Are you sure about this?"

"Reasonably."

"So that's what she found. No wonder they wanted her dead."

"Who, Mr. Carter? Who's 'they'?"

"I don't know. But whoever it was took a stab at killing me earlier today."

"This is madness. We have to go to the authorities. I can tell them everything. I'm not afraid."

"Afraid of what?" Carter said, holding his voice very steady. Tomasson evidently was on to something.

"I think I know who could have wanted Lydia dead. About

a week ago, two members of the Althing Energy Commission came to see me. They said our geothermal energy could be depleting itself. I laughed, of course, but they said the steam vents outside Reykjavik had lessened in intensity. They were having to run the turbines continuously to make up for the loss in power. They said that if something wasn't done soon, the entire city would be in trouble.''

''What else did they say?'' Carter prompted after a moment.

''They were concerned, naturally. But they also seemed worried. Their engineers had studied the problem and concluded that the fissure venting the steam was collapsing very far underground. Nothing that they knew of could be done. They were hiding the information, of course, from the public until they could decide on some alternative plan. That's why they came to the university . . . to me, so quietly. They did not want to arouse any suspicions.'' Again Tomasson fell silent.

''Is there more?'' Carter asked.

''Yes,'' the man replied. ''For a number of years there have been people here who have wanted to develop nuclear power as an alternative energy source. Come into the twentieth century, they say. But it's the big profits they're really interested in. The Energy Commission people were afraid that this decrease in available geothermal energy would help the nuclear proponents. They pleaded with me to do an independent study to see if there wasn't some way to reverse the trend.''

''And you assigned the job to Lydia?''

''Yes,'' Tomasson said. ''There are natural fluctuations in the energy levels. It happens all the time. I thought this was another such event. I didn't think it too important.''

''Lydia got caught in the middle of the political haggling over nuclear power?''

''I'm afraid so.''

''Who are the leaders on this nuclear thing?''

''Members of the Althing. Representatives of Iceland's

big business . . . even members of the Energy Commission.''

"Thorstein Josepsson?''

"Yes,'' Tomasson said. "In fact Josepsson is the leading proponent of the 'nuclear alternative,' as they call it.''

Carter whistled.

"What is it?'' Tomasson asked. He was clearly worried.

"Josepsson was the one who notified me that Lydia was dead. She had been carrying a letter for me in her pocket. He forwarded it. But when I showed up, he seemed very nervous. In fact after I had spoken with him, someone followed me when I went to the university and met you, and while we were talking, my hotel room was entered, my luggage searched, and my personal belongings vandalized.''

"You think Josepsson was responsible?''

"It's possible. As I said, they even tried to kill me about nine hours ago.''

Both men were silent for a few seconds while Carter's mind raced to take in all the implications of what he had been told. Then Tomasson asked, "You say you were followed yesterday?''

"Yes,'' Carter said.

"There was a car behind me all the way in to work this morning,'' Tomasson said. "I thought it odd. But now—''

"Was it a small, black two-door? A Lancia?''

"I don't know the make of the car, but that sounds like it.''

"Go home, Professor. Take the photographs with you, and lock and bolt your doors. I'll be there as fast as I can.''

"But—''

"I think you may be in danger. Please do as I say.''

"This is crazy . . .'' Tomasson said. But he agreed to do as Carter asked. When he hung up, Carter had the operator connect him with police headquarters.

"Captain Einarsson, please,'' he asked the police switchboard operator.

"It's me,'' Carter said when Einarsson came on. "I'm

catching the first flight out for Reykjavik. Any luck on identifying Victor?''

"Not yet," Einarsson said. "I'd like you to stick around for a day or so, though. Until we get this settled."

"Sorry, but that's not possible. I have to get back."

"Something has come up?" Einarsson asked, interested.

"I think so. I'll trade you whatever I find in Reykjavik for whatever you come up with on our friend."

"For now all I can tell you for sure is that he is not an Icelander. We have nothing on him at all."

Carter gave him his number at the Saga Hotel, the only one he knew other than the Borg. When the police captain hung up, Carter sat a moment thinking.

Since he had arrived in Iceland, Einarsson had been the only one who had played it a hundred-percent straight with him. Everyone else seemed to be walking on eggshells, afraid to open up. Everyone seemed to be hiding his own little secrets.

He showered and shaved, packed his single remaining bag, and went downstairs to pay his bill. He took the Land-Rover out to the airport, leaving it in the parking lot. His plane left less than an hour later.

Reykjavik was an eyeful from the air, scrubbed and clean; it reminded him of a bouquet of flowers, the colored houses and gardens so brilliantly clear. It was the air, he thought. In Iceland the air was the clearest he had ever seen it anywhere. Because of the city's unique energy system, there were no smokestacks. No need for power plants to pollute the air. No fireplaces or furnaces in the homes to spread their sulphurous smoke.

Except for one wisp he saw on the south side of the city—a black plume rising like an exclamation point from some unidentifiable source—there was no smoke. A fire, he imagined, then dismissed the thought, his mind preoccupied with Dr. Petur Tomasson.

He landed, looked up the professor's home address in the

phone book, and took a taxi into the city.

Tomasson lived on the south side of the city, and as they were driving, a fire truck, its lights flashing and its siren blaring, screamed past them, and turned in the direction they were headed.

Carter began to have a sinking feeling about this, and he asked the cabbie to speed up.

They turned a second corner, the fire truck still ahead of them, its blue lights pulsing.

Smoke rose in a thick black column over the trees and rooftops. The cabbie said something over his shoulder that Carter couldn't quite catch, and they turned a final time into a narrow lane and pulled up short.

Fire trucks filled the street and many of the yards. Hoses crisscrossed from gutter to gutter. Men with fire hats and slickers ran back and forth while a throng of people watched. In the center of the confusion a two-story house burned like kindling, huge billows of smoke rolling out of its windows.

The cabbie turned. "This is the number you have given me, sir."

"Damn," Carter swore. He jumped out of the cab. "Wait for me," he shouted back at the driver and raced up the street to the crowd.

A thin, middle-aged man in a cardigan and bedroom slippers stood watching. Carter spun him around and shouted, "Did they all get out?"

The man looked at him as if he were crazy.

He pushed his way through the crowd as two firemen came from the rear of the burning house, carrying a body. Ambulance attendants rushed over to them with a stretcher.

Carter broke through the crowd and almost made it to the stretcher-bearers before he was stopped. But he recognized the body. It was Petur Tomasson, badly burned but recognizable. He lay face up, charred pieces of skin hanging from his shrunken cheeks, his lips seared to paper-thinness. It looked as though he were still breathing.

The stretcher-bearers hurried to the ambulance as the

upper story of the house collapsed inward, sending a shower of sparks high into the air. Everyone fell back.

There was nothing more he could do here. He had been too late. The only possibility now was that the professor had hidden the photographs someplace safe and would regain consciousness long enough to tell where they were.

Carter went back to the cab and climbed in the back seat as the ambulance made a U-turn in the narrow lane, and headed away, its sirens screaming.

"Follow that ambulance to the hospital," he said.

The cabbie nodded, made a U-turn, and they hurried back across town to the hospital. Carter paid the driver and hurried up to the waiting area outside the emergency room.

A great many people were coming and going, and after an hour or so, Carter stopped one of the white-coated men and asked about Tomasson.

"I am so sorry, sir. Were you a relative?"

Carter shook his head. "No, just a friend."

"Professor Tomasson passed away within minutes of his arrival here. I am so sorry that you were not informed earlier."

"I see."

"Is there anything I can do?"

Wearily Carter turned away from the doctor. He called a cab, this one to the Saga Hotel, where he checked in. Once he was alone in his room he turned up the heat, ordered himself a bottle of cognac, one glass, no ice or mix, and took a quick shower.

When his bottle came he poured himself a stiff drink, lit a cigarette, and began disassembling and cleaning his gun. He worked slowly, methodically, until every speck of dirt was gone, and it was well oiled and ready for use. Then he disassembled it once more and started all over again.

First Lydia and now Tomasson. How many other innocent people would get hurt before this was stopped?

Of all the evil men in the world, Carter had most often come up against those who betrayed the trust of their public office. Policemen, commissioners, politicians . . . men such as Josepsson.

Around four in the afternoon, his anger somewhat abated, he showered again, got dressed, and went downstairs. An empty cab was waiting in the stand in front of the hotel. Carter got in and asked to be taken to the police station downtown. He was not on assignment here to Iceland. He was not on official business. This incident had gotten too far out of hand; it was time to bring the local police in on it. Let them clean up their own mess.

Police headquarters was housed in a modern building of glass and concrete on the corner of Hverfisgata and Snorrabraut. As Carter got out of the cab and paid his fare, the weak afternoon sun was just tinting the aluminum window casings gold.

Inside, a pretty blond girl behind the information desk looked up and smiled.

"I would like to speak with whoever is investigating the fire this morning near the university," Carter said.

"Have you come for some information, sir?" she asked.

"No, I'm here to give some."

She thumbed through a daily report log. "That would be Sergeant Gundarsson," she said, finding it. "I believe he is still in." She telephoned someone, speaking in rapid-fire Icelandic.

Moments later a young officer in a crisp blue uniform appeared at the corridor door, and Carter followed him through a maze of desks and partitions until they reached a gray, nondescript desk tucked in a corner, where a sallow-faced man, also in a blue uniform, sat typing. Smoke from a cigarette dangling on his lip curled up into his eyes, making him blink from time to time.

"Yes?" he said, looking up.

"I want to talk to you about the fire this morning."

"Tomasson?"

Carter nodded and sat down. "What have you found out?"

"That depends on who you are," Gundarsson said.

"I'm Nick Carter. A friend of Tomasson's—and of his colleague Dr. Lydia Coatsworth, who died here recently."

"I see. And?"

"I think Professor Tomasson was murdered. Arson."

"Faulty gas range in the kitchen, Mr. Nick Carter, American. Who would want to kill the professor?"

"He'd just discovered something very important," Carter said. "Something very important to the internal security of Iceland. I believe he was killed to prevent this information from getting out."

Gundarsson lit another cigarette off the stub of the one in his mouth, then pulled out a pad of paper and a pencil. He jotted down Carter's name. And the names Petur Tomasson and Lydia Coatsworth.

"Go ahead," he said, looking up. "You came to tell me something. Tell it."

Carter began to relate the entire story, nonstop, from the time he'd come to Iceland, just as he had done for Einarsson. It took the better part of thirty minutes for the telling, during which time Gundarsson wrote furiously and smoked continuously. When Carter was done, Gundarsson repeated the main points, Carter made a few corrections, and then the officer rose from his chair, told Carter to wait, and disappeared around a partition.

Carter went over what he had just told the man. Einarsson had been skeptical about the story, but this cop had seemed indifferent. The story sounded lame, of course. Too much speculation and too little hard fact. He should have waited until he had more information. Yet. . . .

Gundarsson came back and took Carter down a long corridor until they reached an office near the end. Gundarsson opened the door, and Carter stepped inside.

The man behind the desk was in shirt-sleeves. Semicircles of sweat appeared under each arm as he put his elbows out in front of him and peered up at Carter through thick, black-rimmed glasses.

"Sit down, Mr. Carter," the man said. His voice was

gruff. A brass nameplate on his desk identified him as Lieutenant Thor Thorsson.

Carter sat down.

"Do you know the time?" the lieutenant asked. He did not seem very happy.

"Four forty-five," Carter said, glancing at his watch.

"My day ends at five, Mr. Carter, at which time our business *will* be concluded, wild stories and all."

"It may seem like a wild story, Lieutenant, but it's true nevertheless."

Thorsson shook his head in exasperation. "I just finished speaking with Mr. Johann Sigurjonsson. On the telephone. He is the gentleman who heads our Energy Commission. He said your story is utter nonsense. There is, and will be in the forseeable future, no shortage of geothermal energy here in Iceland. If Professor Tomasson thought differently, he was wrong."

"They wouldn't admit it. Can you imagine the effect if it became common knowledge that Iceland was running out of power?"

"Mr. Sigurjonsson is lying, then. He heads the biggest business concern in this country, he is a well-known and very respected leader, and he had done a great deal both publicly and privately to benefit dozens of charities. You, on the other hand, are a foreigner. Who shall I believe?"

"I was attacked and nearly killed outside Akureyri by a stranger. Why?"

The cop just glared at him.

"I was getting too close to the truth, and it upset the power in this country. Dr. Coatsworth and Professor Tomasson were on the same story."

"I have had no report from Akureyri yet. Only your ridiculous story."

"Then you will not help me?" Carter asked.

"Drop this immediately," the lieutenant said.

Carter got up and started to leave, but the lieutenant stopped him.

"What hotel are you staying at?"

"The Saga," Carter said. He knew what was coming.

"Do not leave your hotel, Mr. Carter. Reservations on the morning plane to the States will be made for you. Your welcome has expired."

Carter nodded. "I came up here to investigate the accidental death of a friend. Now I am being booted out of the country when I discover it may have been a murder. You people have a strange sense of justice."

"I have also spoken with Mr. Josepsson. He complained about you yesterday. I held off doing anything about it, however, but now you have gone too far."

"So they got to you too," Carter said.

The lieutenant's face turned red. He got to his feet. "One more word . . . just one . . . and you will be spending a very long time in a very unpleasant jail, just downstairs."

Carter nodded after a moment. "I'll be on the morning plane."

"Yes, you will," the lieutenant said.

Outside in the lobby, he asked the girl at the desk if he could glance at the incident report Gundarsson had filed about the fire. She hesitated.

"I've just now spoken with Lieutenant Thorsson about this," he said.

She dug out the report and handed it up. The folder only included one sheet, on which were written the names of Tomasson's estranged wife and their two children. Their address was listed.

He took a cab back to his hotel, and in a phone booth in the lobby he looked up Tomasson's wife. Her last name was not Tomasson. In Iceland, he was learning, there are no last names. One is named for one's father. Tomas's son becomes Tomasson. His daughter, Tomasdottir. Consequently everyone has two names that are his and his alone, no matter who marries whom. Tomasson's wife was Helga Arnadottir. She lived in the eastern sector, Skipholti 33. She was home when he called.

They talked for twenty minutes. She accepted his condolences, and he learned that she and her husband had been on the verge of divorce, and had ceased living together some time ago. She and the professor had two small children, a boy and a girl.

He asked if Tomasson had talked to her at all before he died. Had she seen him during the past few days? Had he perhaps left something in her care?

No. She hadn't talked with him for several weeks.

He thanked her, expressed his sympathies again, and hung up.

As he was crossing the lobby, the desk clerk motioned to him with a folded piece of paper. "A message, sir," he said. "You're to call this number immediately."

It was Einarsson. Carter recognized the Akureyri exchange. He placed the call from his room. Einarsson was in his office.

"Carter?" he shouted.

"Have you got something?"

"We've identified Victor. Turns out Interpol has a file on him several centimeters thick."

"Go ahead."

"Real name is Victor Adolph von Hauptmann. Argentinian."

"Argentinian?"

"Born August 4, 1946, to a German father and an Argentinian mother. Father was Raoul von Hauptmann, German army colonel who managed to escape the fatherland in the last years of the war. Victor didn't show up on the records, however, until December of 1969 when he was picked up in Buenos Aires for disorderly conduct and defacing public property. The arresting officer's jaw was broken. He was jailed several more times over the next year, all for more or less the same thing—inciting to riot, vandalism, disorderly conduct—all of which his father got him out of. But then he disappeared, coming back into the record two years later in Guatemala as a suspect in the shooting deaths of several

Communist guerrillas. He was tried but acquitted. From that point on, it was one thing after another all over Latin America—Chile, Paraguay, El Salvador, even Cuba. Always suspicion of murder or attempted assassination, always on left-wing political figures. Cases brought to trial, then acquittal or charges are dropped when witnesses fail to appear or suddenly change their story. A powerful man . . . or rather, a man with powerful friends.''

"What the hell was he doing in Iceland?'' Carter asked, half to himself.

"I don't know.''

"No mistaking the man?''

"Positive ID. You want me to send you a copy of the report?''

"Not here. I've been kicked out of your country.''

"What?''

"That's right. Josepsson figures if he can't kill me, at least he can have me deported.''

"What happened? Why didn't you call me?''

"Nothing you could have done. But thanks for the thought. Send me the report though, if you would.'' He gave his AXE cover address at Amalgamated Press on Dupont Circle in Washington, D.C. "It will be forwarded to me.''

"I have a feeling I know where you are going,'' Einarsson said.

"If you guess Argentina, you won't be very far off.''

FOUR

High in the building housing the Amalgamated Press and Wire Services, David Hawk looked out his office window at the falling rain and rubbed the back of his neck. The muscles were sore, as was always the case when he was upset, and today he was more upset than usual.

On the desk behind him, a file folder lay open, a field report he had asked his friend, Robert LeMott, the Director of Central Intelligence, to compile for him. It was a thin file, no more than five sheets, comprised of a timetable and a few pages of notes hastily scribbled by LeMott's field m..n, an army colonel in the liaison office at the U.S. base at Keflavik, Iceland. But it was enough to cause Hawk some genuine discomfort.

The file dealt with Nick Carter's activities in Iceland over a forty-eight-hour period during which Nick had managed to get himself shot at and nearly killed, and had stirred up enough ire among the locals to get himself kicked out of the country. At one point he had almost put himself in the position of bringing undue attention to himself as a man with unique and extensive combat training. In short he had almost blown his AXE cover, and this was not to be tolerated.

As Hawk watched, a maroon Jaguar Super America pulled into the parking lot below and glided to a stop. The door

swung open, and Nick Carter got out and hurried through the
rain toward the back door of the building.

Hawk took a cigar out of his pocket, bit off the end, and lit
it. Then he sat down behind his desk to wait.

When Carter opened the door and saw Hawk sitting stiffly
behind his desk, staring directly at him, he knew the old
man's mood was not good. He came in without a word, took a
seat in the winged leather armchair across from the desk, and
guiltily avoided Hawk's gaze.

"You're home quickly," Hawk said dryly. He tapped the
ash from his cigar, then studied the chewed end.

"I was asked to leave Iceland, sir."

"So I've heard," Hawk said gruffly. "Any explanation,
or do I have to guess?"

"I stepped on some toes."

"Sensitive toes?"

"Yes, sir. I think Lydia Coatsworth stepped on the same
toes and was killed for it."

"You were in Iceland as a private citizen, is that not so?
You had no assignment from me, no backup, no license. You
were completely on your own."

"Yes, sir."

Hawk shook his head. Nick could see that the anger was
smoldering in him. "What the hell am I supposed to do?
You've survived a long time in this business."

"Yes, sir?"

"I should think long enough to know that you are not
licensed to act as a private citizen because of the constant risk
of exposure. When you're on duty, and something goes sour,
this office covers for you. Governments are mollified, police
officials cooled down, cover stories strung out. You are
given almost unlimited freedom on your assignments, but
only at a great cost and with the understanding that on your
off-duty time you're not on privilege."

"I know—"

"When you play games with that backup, you leave us

wide open, Carter. Questions are asked, murder investigations begun . . . almost impossible to cover because there was no chance to prepare for these contingencies in advance. I know/you understand this, but it needs to be repeated anyway."

"There were mitigating circumstances," Carter said. Hawk was absolutely correct, of course, but he just couldn't let this go.

Hawk sat back in his chair with a sigh. "I'm willing to listen."

Carter related the story to Hawk just as he had told it to Captain Einarsson and Lieutenant Thorsson before him, except this time no details were left out. He centered his narrative around his suspicions of Thorstein Josepsson, the Althing member with a taste for money and power who, as a former head of the Icelandic Internal Energy Commission, would have the knowledge to run such an operation as Lydia had apparently discovered. He explained Josepsson's position on the commission and how he had lobbied for nuclear power.

Carter added that if he'd had the time, he was sure he could have found financial connections between Josepsson and the contractors who would have done the actual work on whatever machinery was tapping the geothermal energy. Carter was about to go on, pointing out that it was Josepsson who had engineered his ouster from Iceland, when Hawk raised a hand to stop him.

"What you've told me so far is nothing more than a local problem—"

"If I may interrupt, sir," Carter said, "there is something else."

"Important?"

"Yes, sir."

"Go on."

"Just before I left, I spoke with the police captain in Akureyri. My assailant, Victor Hauptmann, was identified as an Argentinian hit man with a long history of rightist politics.

He'd participated in assassinations in Chile, Paraguay, and El Salvador to name a few. A real pro. He had a cyanide capsule implanted beneath the skin of his arm.''

Hawk's attitude changed noticeably. He sat forward and tapped the ash from his cigar. "I haven't heard that used since the war. Strange it should crop up now. Like this."

"I have a feeling Josepsson is fronting for someone else. His people break into my hotel room and cut up my clothes. Eventually they even engineer my persona non grata status. But whoever Josepsson fronts for plays rougher. They killed Lydia and tried with me. Without that explanation, or something like it, Josepsson's actions seem too erratic.''

Hawk nodded in agreement.

"The obvious question," Carter went on, "is who? It may be someone interested in establishing a nuclear plant in Iceland and who is not above importing muscle from a long ways off to keep their secrets secret."

"Argentina?"

Nick nodded.

"You want this as an assignment?"

"Yes, sir," Carter said, relieved. "I think I've discovered something important. But if it turns out to be nothing more than a local flap, we can turn what we have over to the local authorities. I know at least one of them who is straight." Carter hesitated a moment. "But I think there's more to it than that, sir. I think it's international."

Hawk turned and gazed momentarily out the window, his brow knitted. "All right," he said finally. "You know the procedure. I want a complete written report with budget estimates, the works. I'll get Stransky to help you with the figures . . ."

"Begging your pardon, sir, but there really isn't time for that. The trail in Argentina is already getting cold."

Hawk sighed. "Skip the paperwork. Give what you have to Mary, and I'll have Stransky work it up. We'll get the team on it."

"Thank you, sir," Carter said, getting to his feet.

"Do what you have to do. No sense going about this half-assed. But be careful, please."

In the outer office Carter gave Mary the complete rundown on everything that had happened in Iceland. When it was all down on tape, he pecked her on the cheek and left.

The rain had stopped, but the afternoon was chilly. He climbed into his car, drove quickly home, and packed his suitcase. When he was ready he called a cab for the airport.

His flight had left Washington at 6:00 P.M., and twelve hours later he was watching the sun rise over the Rio de la Plata as the vast sprawl of greater Buenos Aires came into view through the ragged clouds.

He had no real idea what he would find here, but he knew that he could not let this go. He kept seeing Lydia's note in his mind's eye. He kept seeing her against the bleak backdrop of Iceland.

The plane dipped south and rumbled to a landing at Ezeiza Airport about thirty miles from the city. Carter deplaned, was passed through customs with no problem, and caught the airport bus into the metropolitan area.

Ever since the Falkland Island war with Britain, the situation here was strained at best. He could see it on the faces of the other passengers, and he kept to himself for the long ride. What he didn't need at this moment was any kind of a stupid incident.

It took nearly forty-five minutes before he got downtown to the Sheraton. He checked in, went upstairs, and when he was cleaned up from the trip, ordered breakfast from room service. Next, he telephoned Juan Mendoza, who was AXE's chief of station here. His cover was political editor for *La Nacion*, and in fact he was one of the most politically knowledgeable men in Argentina.

But Carter had forgotten that business in Buenos Aires rarely begins before ten, and even though it was an hour later here than in Washington, for Argentinians it was still early. Mendoza's wife answered with a few mumbled words thickened with sleep. But Carter's urgent tone brought her awake. Juan was indisposed at the moment, but she promised to have him telephone the hotel immediately.

Room service arrived with his breakfast, and the waiter set the cart by the floor-to-ceiling window where Carter could watch the city come to life. When he was alone he pulled two file folders from his suitcase, poured himself a cup of thick, black coffee, and began to read.

The first was the Interpol file on Victor Hauptmann, and it covered essentially the same ground Einarsson had covered earlier, only in greater detail, with definite dates and places.

The second file was the AXE computer printout of all the reports from other agencies—the CIA, the French SDECE, and the British SIS—on Hauptmann. Most of it consisted of material filed by intelligence agency stations in Bolivia, Uruguay, Venezuela, Panama, and Chile.

On one of the back pages, reference was made to a Paraguay school for assassination. It was a jungle camp run by members of certain security forces and was designed to teach the art of political murder to any with the money to pay for it. The school was reportedly Cuban-staffed and -backed. Hauptmann had apparently attended the school in '69 and '70, and Carter noted with some satisfaction that the encoding for his own career dossier was included in the "see also" listing at the bottom of the page. He remembered the place well. In '78 he had put it out of commission.

Carter was about to pour his third cup of coffee when Mendoza called. He was mildly sarcastic about how nice it was to hear from a man he hadn't seen in two years at practically the crack of dawn, and the two of them traded friendly banter for a few minutes. They had worked together once before on the Venezuelan oil pipeline, having discovered a plot to sabotage it. Ever since that time they had been friends.

"What brings you here, my friend? Business?" Mendoza finally asked. "I didn't see it on the wire."

"Business," Carter said. "Victor Hauptmann. The name ring a bell?"

"You've been traveling in some tough circles if you've been near him, *amigo*. The local toughs call him 'the exterminator.' A very bad man but the best there is for certain types of work."

"Who can afford him lately? Any rumblings?"

"Nothing. It would be doubtful he's working for anyone local. He lives here. He'll keep his nose clean in his own backyard."

"It would be someone with an interest in Iceland."

"Iceland? Are you kidding? What possible connection could there be between Argentina and Iceland? Most of Argentina hasn't heard of the place, much less even know where it is. We've got problems enough with the Maldivas without taking on another island."

"I killed Hauptmann two days ago in a lava field a hundred miles south of the Arctic Circle. The files say he was Argentinian. Someone here must know what he's been up to lately—who he might have been working for."

Mendoza took a while to answer. "It's too bad your boy isn't a Red," he said finally. "We've got Russians crawling all over the place down here. But when it comes to the extreme right, our info is definitely thin."

"I have files on him thick enough to choke a horse, Juan. But not a damn thing on his activities for the past few years. He seemed to have dropped out of sight. And for a man like Hauptmann, that doesn't mean retirement."

"The local police have no love lost for Hauptmann and his kind. They might be able to help."

"Anything else?" Carter asked, somewhat disappointed.

"There is one other source you might try. A kid named José Braga. They say he's phenomenal. A walking computer. He's with the Committee for a Free Argentina, one of our local groups. They keep tabs on all the right-wingers this side of the equator, and Braga keeps it all in his head."

"Too dangerous to keep files?"

"That's what I'm told. This Braga has total recall. If anyone might know where Hauptmann has been and what company he's been keeping, Braga would."

"Where do I find him?"

"That's the hard part. Right now the Committee is on the run. A little mishap with a bomb at a meeting of the conservative party. They're wanted pretty badly just at this moment."

"How do I get to Braga?"

"You might try a priest at St. Dominic's. Father Wilfredo. He's been their spokesman in the past. He hasn't spoken with the police of course, but if you say the right things he might arrange a meeting."

"Thanks."

"Best of luck, *amigo*. You're going to need it with that crowd. The Argentinian Federal Police are very good, and they've had no luck."

"Carter hung up, but only after Mendoza had extracted a promise from him to come out for dinner sometime soon. There was no offer of help. It was AXE policy; agents were to have a certain autonomy unless they requested help or clearly needed it. Juan had just been doing his job.

Using information from the AXE background file, Carter contacted the CIA liaison in the Argentinian Federal Police, a Captain Vargas. Using Vargas's cryptonymn, he asked that any information about Victor Hauptmann be sent to his room at the Sheraton. Vargas, of course, thought Carter was CIA and agreed to do it. Carter didn't like to step on interservice toes this way, but he did not want to go through a lot of lengthy explanations at the moment. If the kid Mendoza had mentioned could not be found, he was evidently good. If the waters got too muddied around Carter, Braga might go deeper.

While he was waiting, Carter took a leisurely shower and shaved. He was just finishing putting on a sport jacket to hide Wilhelmina nestled under his arm, when he heard a knock at the door. He opened it to find a well-groomed young man in a crisp uniform standing in the corridor. He handed Carter a fat manila envelope, saluted stiffly, and left.

Vargas had worked very fast. Incredibly fast, as a matter of fact.

Carter brought the envelope over to the window where he

sat down and took out the file folder stuffed with papers. It was an old file, however, its information no more up-to-date than the things he already had. It was disappointing. The *federales*, it seemed, knew even less about Hauptmann than Washington did, although he did uncover one interesting fact.

Hauptmann's mother had been Argentinian, but his father had been German. His father had come here just after the war and had set up a small printing business. The business had failed, there had been a divorce, and the father had eventually returned to Germany. He knew all that. What was new was that apparently Hauptmann's father had been an officer in the SS. The notation after the name was nothing more than the two letters, faded now with time, and yet it was something Washington did not have.

Carter closed the file and put it with the others in his suitcase. Then he went out, locking the door behind him. Outside he caught a cab.

St. Dominic's was a small church that looked as though it had seen better times. The pink stucco had fallen from the bricks in several places, and its plain wooden door looked well worn. But the sign in front was freshly painted, and as Carter's cab pulled up and he got out, the bells were ringing out the hour.

The church was located in the western end of the city, nestled in with the *villas miserias*—cities of misery—the slums made up of corrugated cardboard, tin, and plywood shanties pushed together in an incredible jumble. A group of filthy dirty, ragged children begging for coins surrounded Carter as he stepped from the cab. *Norteamericanos* were very rare in this part of the city. He took the change from his cab fare, added a few pesos, and distributed it among them. Then he went inside.

At the altar a man was lighting candles. Carter walked down the aisle and, when the priest was finished, cleared his throat.

"Father Wilfredo?"

The old man turned around. The sagging, lined flesh of his face bunched around his eyes as he squinted at Carter in the near darkness. "Yes, my son?"

"I would like to speak with you, Father, if I may. It is something of very great importance," Carter said in Spanish.

"*Momento, por favor,*" Father Wilfredo said. "Please sit down. I will be finished in a moment."

The priest turned back to his candles, and Carter took a seat in the first row of pews. He waited until the priest had lit all the candles, then several more minutes while the man knelt in front of the crucifix and prayed.

Slowly the old man got up, shuffled to the vestry to the left of the altar, and a few minutes later reappeared wearing street clothes and a clerical collar. He eased himself into the pew next to Carter.

"And now, what may I do for you?"

"I am looking for a young man, Father. José Braga. I was told you might be able to help."

The smile left the old man's face. "There are many looking for José. Half of Argentina would like to find him. Why do you want to see him? You are American?"

Carter nodded. "I want to speak with him because he might have knowledge of a man I'm looking for. A man who is a hired killer."

The priest looked at him closely.

"I would be willing to pay well."

The priest sighed. "He needs money. There is so little food. If you can be trusted. Who is this man you seek?"

"Victor Hauptmann. I must know where he has been, who he has been working for, and what he has been doing for the past year. The information is worth a lot to me. Perhaps as much as one thousand dollars."

The old eyes looked at him uncertainly. "If I deliver your message, what would stop you from telling the police?"

"I am not from the police. I have no interest in them nor in what they think José Braga might be involved in. Victor

Hauptmann tried to kill me several days ago. I have reason to believe he killed a very good friend of mine. A woman. I want to know why. I want to know who he is working for. Carter took out two hundred-dollar bills and handed them over. "One is for José, and one is for the church. There will be more when I have spoken with him."

Father Wilfredo glanced doubtfully at the money in his hand.

"I will meet him anywhere at any time. He can pick the place. And I will come alone."

Father Wilfredo looked Carter directly in the eye, weighed the alternatives for a moment, then put the money in his jacket pocket. "Come back after the eleven o'clock mass," he said.

It was a few minutes after noon when the last of the few parishioners had cleared the church. Carter came forward. The old priest said nothing. He turned and walked toward the rear of the building. Carter followed.

They went through a narrow door concealed in the wood paneling behind the altar, into an ill-lit hall, and finally into a tiny room at the back. Floor-to-ceiling bookcases jammed with papers and books covered three of the walls. A battered, ancient armchair and footstool stood to one side, and in the center of the bare, tiled floor was set a squat, ornate wooden desk. Perched upon the desk as though he too were a part of the furnishings was a slight, dark boy in threadbare cotton trousers and shirt. On his upper lip was a very thin mustache. He looked like any other Argentinian teenager except that across the bridge of his nose rested a pair of thick glasses that enlarged his eyes, giving him a vaguely owlish appearance.

"José Braga?" Carter asked.

The boy nodded, watching Carter suspiciously. The priest walked behind the boy and put his hand protectively on his shoulder.

"The money," Braga demanded.

Carter pulled out nine one-hundred-dollar bills and handed them to the boy who looked at them, then handed the money to the priest.

"You have just saved the lives of my comrades in arms, and you have prolonged the valiant struggle of the Argentinian people against the oppression of its cruel imperialist government."

Carter noticed the boy did not speak the usual street jargon, and glancing at the book-lined walls, he could see why. Although his phrases were trite, they were well spoken.

"If the speechmaking is over, I came here for information," Carter said. The boy and the priest exchanged glances.

"What do you want to know about the pig Hauptmann? He has disappeared," Braga snapped.

"I killed him," Carter said.

Braga's eyes widened. "No one deserved death more than that maniac. But why did you do such a thing?"

"He tried to kill me."

The boy's eyes narrowed. "And now you want more information about him. What sort of information?"

"Where was he six months ago?"

"In jail. Salto, Uruguay. He had a profitable little gun-running business across the Uruaguay River into Concordia until his boat developed troubles and he was stranded."

"I have looked at the police files. That wasn't included."

Braga shrugged. "Communications are not always good with the provinces. And relations are somewhat strained with Uruguay at the moment." He smiled as though he'd had a hand in straining the relations himself.

"How do you know this, about Hauptmann?"

"You doubt my word, *señor*?"

Carter held his silence.

"We sent a man to Salto with orders to kill Hauptmann. He has been a thorn in our sides. He was to be arrested and put into the cell next to our man. Then a knife was to be slipped between the pig's ribs while everyone slept. It was all arranged. But then Hauptmann escaped."

"How? Did he have help?"

Again the boy shrugged, a loose, careless gesture that Carter was beginning to find irritable. "The man with the monocle."

"Who?"

"He is a European. He is always there when Hauptmann or men like him need help. Buys their way out of jail if possible, or shoots their way out."

This was something new. Carter had not seen anything about such a man in AXE files.

"I've never seen the man, but others have. They said his eye behind his monocle is as cold as the winter wind. He is said to have no heart."

"A name?"

Braga shook his head.

"How about your man . . . the one you sent to Salto to kill Hauptmann? Perhaps he saw this European? Perhaps he can give me a description?"

The priest crossed himself. "Pepé Morales is dying. Cancer. There is not much time."

"Did he see him?"

"I don't know," Braga said. "When he came back he was sick. He didn't say anything. We didn't ask."

"I would like to ask him. It is very important," Carter said.

Braga started to say no, but the priest held him off. They went out into the corridor for a minute or two, and when the door opened again, the boy was gone.

"It is best this way," Father Wilfredo said.

"That was easy money," Carter said bitterly.

"It was all he knew, believe me. But I will tell you how to get to Pepé. Perhaps he will be able to help you," the priest said. "He is back in Salto, there is a cantina . . ."

During the cab ride back to his hotel, Carter vacillated between wanting to disbelieve what he had been told and wondering if Braga hadn't been straight with him after all. It was possible that neither AXE nor the CIA, nor Interpol, nor even the Argentine Federal Police had any idea Hauptmann was in jail. It was also possible that another organization could have found out—if Hauptmann had sent out word—and decided to buy Hauptmann's freedom in return for services rendered.

When he reached his hotel he made arrangements to rent a car. Twenty minutes later they brought it around, a white '67 Chevrolet with eighty thousand miles on the odometer. It looked rough, but the tires were good and it was reasonably clean.

Another half an hour of haggling produced the necessary insurance and registration papers, and he was on his way northward on the Avenida Eduardo Maredo with a road map open on the seat beside him.

Salto was a two-hundred-mile trip, but the roads were good, and by five forty-five that afternoon he had stopped for directions to the cantina the priest had told him about. By six he was parking in front of the place, which was just off the square in a very sleepy, dusty little village with only one main street. The square held an open-air market.

There were very few people about, and the cantina seemed to be closed, so Carter went over to one of the stalls in the market, where a man was just bundling up his pots and pans.

He looked up hopefully.

"Do you know a man who is very sick named Pepé Morales?" Carter asked. He pulled out a few pesos.

The man looked Carter over. He eyed the money, but he made no move to reach for it.

Carter sensed the mistrust. "Father Wilfredo from St. Dominic's in Buenos Aires sent me. He said I could find Pepé here."

The man nodded slowly and pointed down a side street. "The last house," he said. "In the back." His Spanish was very thick, very difficult to understand.

Carter handed him the money, then went back to his car. From his things in the trunk, he pulled out a thin, black briefcase containing a portable Identi-Kit. He had brought it along on a hunch, and he hoped it was about to pay off. He drove up the narrow street.

The house was little more than a dirt-floored shack. Carter knocked at the door.

"Who is it?" a woman asked impatiently.

"I have come to see Pepé."

"Go away!"

Carter gently pushed open the door. The light was dim, but in the darkness he could make out a mattress on the floor. A man was lying there, an old woman bent over him. The whites of her eyes flashed up at him.

"Go away!"

"I am sorry, but I must speak with him. It is very urgent."

The woman began to struggle to her feet, but the man reached up, gently laying his hand on her arm, stopping her. "It doesn't matter," he said softly.

The woman stood, and with a furious look retired to the other side of the room.

Carter crouched beside the man on the mattress. "Are you the one they call Pepé?"

"Yes," the man said, his voice hoarse and soft.

"José Braga sent me. He says you were the man in prison with Victor Hauptmann."

Pepé nodded. His breathing was labored. He was obviously in great pain.

"A man came to get him out of the prison. The man with the monocle. Did you see him? Did you see his face that night? Clearly?"

Pepé nodded again.

"I must find this man with the monocle. Hauptmann is dead, but I must find his friend. Do you understand?"

Tears leaked from the man's eyes. But once again he nodded his understanding.

"I need this man's description, and I have something with me that will help." Carter opened the briefcase and took out a notebook with interchangeable plastic pages. The overlays were divided into sections, each section containing a facial feature of a different type. By flipping the various pages back and forth, and by interchanging the proper overlays, one could put together almost any combination of features.

"Do you feel up to helping me?"

Pepé's face was grayish-white. He lay with his mouth open, his lips white and dry, his eyes narrowed to slits. "Yes," he whispered.

"Do you have a lamp?" Carter asked the woman.

She lit a kerosene lamp and brought it over. Carter set it on the floor and propped the notebook on his knee. "Was he bald?" he asked. "Short hair? Shorter than this? And the nose, long or short?"

The process took three-quarters of an hour. Carter worked steadily, not wanting to rush the dying man but fully aware that the man's strength was limited. What began as nods and shakes of the head became, after a time, little more than eye movements and an occasional grunt toward the end. Nevertheless, a picture began to take shape.

Carter's quarry turned out to be apparently a large man whose head was either shaved or naturally bald. He was thickly built with ridges of muscle along his bull neck. His face was squarish, the mouth grim, the eyes blue and penetrating. He was about sixty, perhaps a bit more or less.

When they were done, Pepé was completely exhausted. He lay with his eyes closed, his breath coming more irregularly than before. He opened his mouth to speak, but the words were too faint to be heard.

"Do you know what he's trying to say?" Carter asked the woman. He felt a great amount of pity for these people, but there was little if anything he could do for them.

She came over and knelt down beside the mattress. Pepé spoke again. She looked up. "He wants to know who you are," she said. "He wants to know if you will kill this man."

Carter crouched back down and looked into Pepé's eyes. "I think this man is trying to have me killed. I may have to kill him."

"Good," Pepé croaked. Then he closed his eyes and appeared to fall asleep.

Carter got slowly to his feet. "Has he seen a doctor?"

"Who has money for such things?" the woman snapped.

Carter put the Identi-Kit composite back in the briefcase. Then he pulled out several hundred dollars and held it out to the woman. But she did not reach out to take it, so Carter put it on the floor beside Pepé.

"When he wakes up, thank him for me. He has been a very big help."

"Swine!" the woman hissed.

Outside, the sun was low in the sky, and shadows around the little hut were beginning to lengthen. He walked to the car and was about to pull the door open when he noticed a small smear of grease near the front wheel well. Odd, he thought. He'd inspected the car thoroughly before he'd driven up here. He didn't remember any grease.

He got in, put the key in the ignition but didn't turn it. Directly ahead, through the windshield, the rutted mud road that led back to town lay silent in the gathering haze of twilight. A pair of trees bobbed at the end of the lane. To his right were the cluttered backyards of several neighboring families. They had been busy centers of activity when he came—children playing, women hanging wash. Now the children were gone, and the wash was down. Not dry. Not yet.

Quiet, he thought. Much too quiet.

Slowly he reached down and pulled the door latch. As the door popped, he hit it with his shoulder and dove headfirst into the dirt. He'd no more than cleared the seat when a shot sounded. The windshield went white with cracks, and there was a saw-toothed hole where his head had been.

An automatic weapon opened fire from a hedge about sixty yards down the road. Carter rolled frantically back and forth as the chattering slugs kicked up dirt all around him.

Carter rolled under the car as the barrage continued. The bullets clattered into the metal on all sides, and he could hear the windshield breaking up.

The hedge was located directly down the road from the car. Carter drew his Luger and pumped a few rounds toward the spot, but the firing continued. Whoever it was seemed to have an inexhaustible supply of ammunition.

Then he saw two wires leading down from the engine compartment, and he suddenly realized what he should have understood earlier. The wires ended in a lump of plastique directly beneath the seat on the driver's side. The machine gunner had been nothing more than insurance.

The bullets kept coming, pinning Carter down. It was as if the gunman were trying to pick the car apart and detonate the bomb himself.

The first two wires were connected to the ignition switch. He pulled down one, then the other, being very careful not to let their ends make contact. Then he wrapped the first wire around the coils of the right front wheel spring, leaving its end exposed. He did the same with the second, wrapping it around a lower coil in the spring and fanning its end; when the spring was compressed, the ends would meet and the bomb would explode. Then he pulled himself on his elbows out from under the car's rear bumper.

The firing stopped for a moment or two, and Carter ducked around to the passenger side of the car, threw open the door, and scrambled inside.

The firing did not resume.

Carter reached up and put the car in neutral, then turned on the ignition. The wires on the springs below were hot now, the bomb activated.

Making sure the steering wheel was straight, the car pointing directly at the line of hedges, Carter turned the ignition again, starting the car. He slipped the gear lever into drive, and as the car began to move, he slid backward out of the car and rolled away from the rear wheels.

The firing started again as the car gathered speed, lumbered down the road, and hit the ditch near the hedges. The explosion blew out its doors like a pair of wings, and the car burst into flames, glass, bits of hot metal, and burning upholstery raining down.

Carter leaped up and ran toward the hedges, expecting to see the gunman making a run for it. But the area around the car was burning, making it impossible to see much of anything beyond.

A motorcycle engine kicked into life, and Carter turned in time to see a man with an automatic rifle strapped to his back bouncing over the terrain. Carter brought up his Luger and fired twice, but it was no use; the figure was well out of range.

He holstered his gun after a bit, then went back to the house to check on Pepé and his woman, who had been badly frightened by the barrage of gunfire. Once again, the little street was silent.

FIVE

Twenty-four hours later, Carter was back in Buenos Aires in the suburb of San Isidro, sitting at the dinner table in Juan Mendoza's apartment. Mendoza, his wife Evita, and Carter had just finished eating a thick slice of Argentinian Pampa-bred tenderloin. During the meal, Carter had described the murder attempt in Salto. He had checked on Pepé, who was sleeping peacefully, and then had gotten out of there on foot before the police came. It wasn't until early morning that he was able to hitch a ride from a farmer to the border and then to a railway station.

The cook came in to clear the dishes, and Evita Mendoza excused herself to follow her back into the kitchen to see about dessert, leaving Carter and Mendoza alone at the table. Mendoza pulled his chair back, pulled out two thick Panatellas, and offered one to Carter.

"What makes you so sure it wasn't simply a random act of terrorism against a Yankee?" Mendoza asked, reaching over with a match to light Carter's cigar.

Carter puffed several wisps of pale smoke. "Terrorists might have planted the bomb, but they would not have waited around with a gunman to make sure the bomb did its job. It was definitely a determined killer. A man with a very specific target: me."

"You think the attack was connected somehow to this business in Iceland?"

"Whoever it was, knew I had just come in. They followed me up to Salto."

"But how?"

"A leak. Maybe in your organization here. Maybe in the CIA's. It may be Captain Vargas in the Federal Police. I borrowed one of his files."

Mendoza thought a moment. "It would take quite an organization to keep tabs on you from Iceland to Washington and then down here."

"Yes."

This last prospect seemed to make Mendoza uncomfortable. "All right," he said, pulling his chair in closer and spreading his hands palms-down on the table. "Let's examine what you've come up with so far. Someone in Iceland, you say, is manipulating things so that a nuclear power plant will be built up there. Why? What would that get them?"

"I don't know," Carter said. "That part's got me stumped."

"At this moment whoever is running the show has ties here in Argentina. They hired a local to make a try on you in Iceland, and now that you're here, they've tried again."

"They've been watching me, and they want me dead. They'll try again."

"But who? I keep coming back to that, Nick. No one in Argentina has the resources to build a nuclear power plant under such secrecy. We would have heard about it by now. It takes a very big organization and a lot of capital to keep something like that so totally private."

"Maybe the man with the monocle has the answers."

"Him." Mendoza spat the word. "Do you still have the sketch?"

Carter unfolded the sheet on which he'd transferred the features of the portrait Pepé had helped him put together in Salto and handed it across to Mendoza.

Mendoza studied the rendering for several silent moments. Then he looked up. "This almost looks like Marc Ziegler."

"Who is that?"

"A friend of mine from the San Isidro Tennis and Sport Club. He lives not too far from here."

"What does he do?"

"He's head of a very large conglomerate. Hemispheric Technologies. They have their headquarters south of the city."

Carter didn't say anything.

Mendoza glanced again at the picture, then up at Carter. "You're not suggesting . . ."

"Why not?" Carter said.

"He's a good man, Nick. I can't imagine he'd be mixed up in murder. Besides, his company is involved with computers, not reactors."

Carter shrugged. "Ziegler is German, I assume. Josepsson was dealing with Germans. I met two of them in Iceland."

"That's not fair, Nick. There are a lot of Germans here in Argentina."

"Some of them former Nazis on the run. In Hauptmann's file there was a notation that his father had been in the S.S. I wonder what Ziegler's file looks like?"

"The police wouldn't have one on him, I wouldn't think. We surely do not."

Carter sat back, puffing his cigar as he tried to think this out. There was every possibility that he was chasing wild geese. Yet. . . . He looked up. "Who's the Israeli ambassador to Argentina?"

"David Lieb."

"Do you know him?"

Mendoza nodded. "As a matter of fact I did an article on him and his family. 'The Changing Face of Israel' it was called."

"Will he remember you?"

"Certainly. The article appeared not very long ago. He sent me a case of Dom Perignon."

"Call him. Tell him you may have come across some information on Nazi war criminals, and you want to know to whom you should pass it."

Reluctantly Mendoza made the call. Lieb was just getting

home from an evening at the theater. He was not happy about being disturbed, but when Mendoza made it clear what he wanted, Lieb's attitude suddenly changed.

"Roger Seidman. He is my political consul. He would be most interested to hear what you might have." He gave a telephone number.

"Mossad, I'm sure of it," Carter said. "Call him."

Mendoza placed the call, and when it was answered, Carter took the phone.

"Mr. Seidman?"

"Yes," a man answered cautiously.

"My name is Nick Carter. I am with the American State Department. We have run across some interesting information here in Argentina concerning certain Nazi war criminals."

"I'm sorry, Mr. Carter, but I don't know how I can be of any help . . ."

"Your name and telephone number were given to my associate just minutes ago by David Lieb. He suggested you might be able to help."

"I see," Seidman said, still wary.

"Does the name Marc Ziegler mean anything to you?"

There was a slight hesitation. "Come to my office in the embassy first thing in the morning. Let's say nine."

"We'll be there."

At precisely 9:00 A.M., Carter and Mendoza were ushered into Roger Seidman's office on the second floor of the Israeli embassy.

Seidman was a small, balding man with a ridge of black curly hair that fit his head like a crown. He invited them to take seats across from his huge desk in the book-lined office. The window was open to the lovely morning.

"I have checked with your State Department, Mr. Carter, but no one there has heard of you," Seidman said. He seemed amused.

"An oversight."

"I suspect that you are with one of the intelligence agencies."

"Does it matter?" Carter asked.

After a moment Seidman smiled. "No. Our common interest seems to be a man you call Marc Ziegler."

Carter took out the composite sketch and passed it across. Seidman looked at it, then handed it back. "Except for a monocle, this man is Marc Ziegler. How did you come by his name and this drawing?"

Mendoza had winced at the identification. But he said nothing.

Carter quickly related his story, beginning with the mysterious death of Lydia Coatsworth and ending with the attempt on his own life outside the town of Salto. He left out any reference to AXE, the CIA, or the police files he had been privy to.

Seidman listened attentively, his hands folded on the desk in front of him, showing little or no emotion. When Carter was finished, he took out a pack of dark brown Israeli cigarettes and lit one after first offering the pack around.

"You have, of course, heard of the Odessa, Mr. Carter?" he asked, exhaling a small cloud of foul-smelling smoke.

Carter just nodded. He did not want to reveal too much of his own knowledge before he had heard what the man was going to tell him.

"It is the organization of former S.S. officers . . . the animals who were responsible for the death camps across Europe in which six million of my people were slaughtered. They have been in open hiding since after the war. They have a very large, very powerful organization, very wealthy from gold stolen from . . . the bodies . . . of their victims." Seidman stopped for a moment.

"The organization is real, then."

"Very," Seidman shot back. "Just after the war, they used their money to set up underground railroads to ferry themselves and their kind out of Europe, and to provide new identities, new positions, and a new life in friendly countries

. . . such as Argentina, where they could be assured of no extradition.''

"And nowadays?'' Carter asked.

"The Odessa is stronger than ever, but now it has two goals: the first is to protect its own from continued inquiries; and the second is to take advantage of the enormous wealth they stole and the investments this wealth has yielded to promote the cause of the Third Reich.''

Mendoza had held himself erect through all that, not saying a word, but now he leaned slightly forward. "Mr. Seidman, we came here to discuss Marc Ziegler. What can you tell us about him?''

"We think he is a member of the Odessa.''

The breath went out of Mendoza. "I know him personally.''

"Yes, I know that,'' Seidman said.

"Are you certain?'' Carter asked.

"Reasonably,'' Seidman said. "If we are correct, then Ziegler is one of the organization's ranking members. We believe he was General Martel Zimmermann during the war. Worked for Himmler himself. He came out in March of 1944 as one of the youngest generals of the Reich.''

"But you've done nothing?''

Seidman shrugged. "We'd very much like to get our hands on him, Mr. Carter, but until he leaves the country under our eyes, or commits some crime against Argentine law, we can do nothing. We do not have proof needed, and even if we did, the Argentine government would rather not act, especially against someone so rich. We've considered kidnapping the man, but since the Eichmann thing, that has become impossible.''

"What would the Odessa—providing Marc Ziegler is the man you think he is—want in Iceland?'' Carter asked.

"I don't know,'' Seidman said. "But it is of extreme interest to us. He may be getting ready to make some move. We've gotten the feeling that he's getting anxious. He may be feeling hemmed in here. We think he may be planning something . . . exactly what, we don't know.''

Carter got to his feet. Seidman jumped up. "But we are not done here . . .''

"I'm afraid we are,'' Carter said. "I gave you what information I had, and you confirmed my suspicions.''

"Your suspicions about what? How did Ziegler's name come up in connection with the trouble in Iceland? And just who are you?''

Mendoza had gotten to his feet as well. He shook hands with Seidman. "Thank you for your assistance.''

Carter shook Seidman's hand. "If I come up with anything significant, I'll let you know,'' he said, and he and Mendoza left the office.

When they were gone, Seidman sat back down behind his desk, stubbed out the cigarette, and picked up the phone.

"There are two men leaving my office,'' he told his assistant. "I want them followed.''

The middle-class houses of Belgrano, a suburb on Buenos Aires's south side, slipped past as Mendoza talked. He was driving.

"I don't know about these Israelis,'' he said. "They act as if Odessa is the most important thing in the world to them, but then they let us walk out of there just like that.''

"We haven't heard the last of them,'' Carter said.

"We will regret they are involved.''

"It was the quickest, surest way I knew of getting information on Ziegler. And we are on the same side, you know.''

Mendoza pulled his Fiat onto the shoulder at the edge of a huge, well-tended piece of property. A large office building rising out of the center of the acreage seemed to be constructed entirely of gold-tinted windows.

"That's it,'' Mendoza said.

The building looked like a huge block of bullion set in a thicket of lush greenery.

"Computers, not nuclear reactors, Nick. I think both you and Seidman are way off.''

"We'll see," Carter said absently. "Let's go to the front gate and see what kind of a rise we can get out of them."

They continued down the highway, turning into the long, blacktopped driveway that was blocked by a gate and a small guardhouse.

One of the guards came out. *"Buenos dias, señores,"* the guard said. "Your names and your business, please."

"Howdy, partner," Carter said, leaning over toward the driver's window. "I'm Nick Carter with Techtelco. We're a small outfit out of Beaumont, Texas. I'm here to have a parlez-vous with Mr. Ziegler."

The guard checked his clipboard list. "I do not show an appointment for you, sir," he answered in English.

"Impossible," Carter drawled. "Marc specifically said eleven o'clock sharp on the eighteenth."

"But, *señor*, this is the seventeenth."

"Is that right? Missed it by a whole day, have I? Well, you just squeeze us in somewhere. It's real important I palaver with the man."

"But, *señor*, there are company rules—"

"Hang the rules, boy! Marc Ziegler is making an offer to buy my company. I either see him today or it's no deal. And that's final."

The guard was flustered. "Excuse me a moment, *señores*," he said, and he disappeared back into the guardhouse. A minute later he reappeared. "Mr. Ziegler is not in his office, and his personal secretary cannot be disturbed. You must understand that there is no way in which I can confirm—"

"Well, the hell with it!" Carter said. "You just let us through, and we'll wait for him inside."

Mendoza started the car, and the disconcerted guard quickly lifted the barrier as they passed through. A few hundred yards up the driveway they turned into a visitors' parking lot.

"It won't take them very long to find us out," Mendoza said, turning off the engine and pocketing the keys.

"You stay here," Carter said. "If there's any trouble, run like hell." He grabbed a notebook and papers from the back seat.

"Be careful with that," Mendoza said. "I've spent a lot of hours researching that article."

"I'll be right back with it," Carter said. He got out of the car, left the parking lot, crossed the road, and hurried up the long steps to the front door.

The receptionist at the information desk was busy talking to a young man in shirt-sleeves. Carter walked up to her, out of breath.

"Important personal delivery for Señor Ziegler," he said in Spanish, holding out the papers.

The girl glanced up. "Elevator is down the hall," she said, pointing to the left. "Señor Carlos is his personal secretary. See him."

Carter nodded and hurried off in that direction.

Ziegler's office suite was behind a set of glass doors on the twelfth floor. Behind a long desk in the front sat an absolutely stunning young woman with long dark hair, wide dark eyes, and a lithe, sensuous figure. She was busy typing.

"I'm here to see Mr. Ziegler," Carter announced in English, coming up to her desk.

She scrutinized him closely. "You are the man from the front gate, aren't you?" she asked in charmingly accented English. "The one they called up about?" She smiled. "Just what is it you want?" She was lovely. Her complexion was flawless. But there was just a hint of sadness in her eyes, which made her even more appealing.

"Do you really want to know?" he asked, his Texas drawl more pronounced. "I came to see you, darlin'."

She laughed. "You're in big trouble, you know."

A retailer's plastic bag sat on the floor next to her chair. He could read the name of the boutique on the bag.

"I saw you at Armando's. I told them I had to know more about you. They gave me your name and told me that you worked here." The embossed nameplate on her desk read

Roberta Redgrave. A very un-Argentinian name.

"Are you serious?" she asked. Her voice was lovely.

"Very," Carter said. He was very conscious of the time.
He didn't have much of it left. "It cost quite a few American
dollars to find out about you. And I don't intend to let you get
away easily. I want to take you to dinner."

She was amused and slightly breathless. "I can't believe
you're serious."

"I had to find out if you were as lovely face-to-face as you
were at a distance. You are."

Shaking her head incredulously, she picked up the desk
phone and started to dial.

"Please," he said, reaching across and putting his finger
on the button. "At least give me a chance. I took a lot of risks
coming up here like this. Just have dinner with me. Afterward, if you still don't like me, I won't ever bother you
again."

"I don't even know you."

"Then have lunch with me first. Can't be any harm in that.
Broad daylight. What time are you free?"

"One," she said automatically.

"I'll be waiting," Carter said, smiling. "But where? Pick
a place. Something nice."

"Tomo Uno. It's not far from here."

"I'll be there at one. A date?"

She sighed and finally nodded. "Just lunch," she said.

He backed away from the desk. "If you don't come, I'll
return and camp on your desk," he threatened.

She laughed again, somewhat dazed. He was almost out to
the doors before she called after him. "But what is your
name?"

"Nick Carter," he said.

From the end of the hall the guard from outside appeared,
leading an entourage of smilarly dressed security men. Carter
ducked around a corner and into a door marked *Escalera*. He
took the stairs down a flight, then slipped out onto the
eleventh floor, where he caught the elevator.

There was a lot of commotion on the main floor, but no one seemed to notice him as he slipped out the front doors, hurried across the driveway to the parking lot, and jumped in next to Mendoza.

"Find out anything . . ." Mendoza started to ask.

"Move!" Carter snapped.

Mendoza started the car and peeled out of the parking lot, tires squealing. There were several security men at the main gate, but Mendoza did not slow down as he drove up on the grass and around the barrier. Soon they were back out on the highway, heading as fast as the car would go back into the city.

"Will they follow us?" Mendoza asked.

"I don't think so," Carter said, sitting back. He had entered Ziegler's territory to shake him up, nothing more. Instead he had accomplished something much better . . . or at least he had set the wheels in motion.

Carter told Mendoza what had happened in Ziegler's outer office, and then he had his friend drop him off at a car rental place downtown, where he hired an Audi 5000.

He drove out to Tomo Uno from directions he had been given at the rental office. It turned out to be an obviously expensive restaurant. Roberta had very good taste.

They were just setting up for the heavy afternoon crowd when Carter walked in. He found the headwaiter and for fifty dollars assured himself personalized service par excellence. He made his selections from the menu then and there, then retired to the bar where he ordered a cognac and called a florist.

He started by ordering two dozen roses, but then he thought better of it. He was a very rich Texan, about to strike it even richer. He splurged.

The flowers, two vans full of them, arrived a scant forty-five minutes later, and by the time they'd finished setting everything up, an entire corner of the main dining room was a wall-to-wall rose garden.

He sat waiting in the midst of it all, fielding stares from the other diners and the restaurant help, until 1:20 when he saw her wending her way through the tables behind the head-waiter. When she saw the flowers, her jaw dropped.

"Oh, my God," she whispered.

Carter had gotten to his feet and held a chair for her, but for several embarrassingly long seconds she stood where she was.

He had lost her, he thought. But at that moment the customers in the restaurant all got to their feet and began to applaud. Romance was alive and well in Argentina.

Carter smiled and bowed gallantly, and Roberta, awed by the entire scene, sat dumbly in the chair he was holding.

When the room had finally quieted and the other patrons had returned to their meals, she leaned across the table and whispered hoarsely, "You're crazy."

"Absolutely," Carter said, laughing. "That's how I got where I am today."

"And where is that?"

Carter told her about Techtelco of Beaumont, Texas, making it up as he went along, and surprising himself by coming up with a very credible cover under such short notice. Meanwhile, the waiter served the first course, a shrimp scampi in wine sauce, and they began to eat. This was the major meal of the day for many Argentinians.

He began slowly drawing her out. Her last name, Redgrave, was after her English mother, she explained. Her father had been German, a real bastard. When her parents got divorced, she legally changed her name to her mother's maiden name.

She was charming and very bright. She had gone to the university here in Buenos Aires but had spent some time with an aunt in England.

Several times he tried to gently steer the conversation toward Ziegler, but each time she resisted, saying she was not allowed to talk about business outside the office.

They talked about other things during the rest of the meal.

After dessert, when they were having coffee and brandy, Carter tried once more.

"I saw his portrait in the office," Carter said. "Ziegler looks too stern. Old school. Too much work."

"He is a difficult man. A workhorse. Day and night, I sometimes think. Always meeting someone. Always flitting here or there."

Carter sipped his brandy.

She looked at her watch. "I must get back," she said, suddenly getting up.

"I'll drive you back," Carter said.

"No, you stay. I have my own car outside." She looked at all the flowers. "Crazy," she said, looking at him. "But lovely."

"Will I see you again?" Carter asked. "Dinner?" He didn't want to lose her now, but he did not want to push.

She took a card out of her purse and laid it on the table. "Tonight," she said. "Ten o'clock. I'll fix a special dinner."

She started to go but then turned back. "By the way, Nick, I've had that bag from Armando's for two months now . . . since the last time I shopped there."

SIX

The address on the card turned out to be a highrise in the center of town off Avenida Callao, overlooking the Plaza del Congresso. Roberta Redgrave's apartment was on the seventh floor.

She answered his knock wearing a peasant blouse richly embroidered around the neckline and a simple skirt that flared out away from her lovely legs. Her cheeks were flushed.

"Fix yourself a drink, and make yourself comfortable," she said. "I'm just about finished in the kitchen."

It was a small apartment. A table for two was set in one corner. A slender candle burned in its center. He threw off his jacket, poured himself a small cognac from a sideboard, and sat down in an easy chair. "Need any help in there, darlin'?" he asked.

"No, thank you," she called from the other room.

In a few minutes she appeared bearing a casserole dish with pot holders. He jumped up and helped her straighten the trivet to put it on, then, when they were seated, he poured two glasses of a very pale red wine.

"Considering the meal we had at lunch, I did not think you would be terribly hungry," she said, serving him. "This is just something light."

It was *pesce d'ananasso*, a mixture of broiled fish, noodles, and fresh pineapple. He had had it before at a fine restaurant in Rome. The dish before him was more than equal to it. And he told her so.

"Thank you," she said. "You worked hard chasing me; I thought I might try the same."

Roberta seemed even more enchanting by candlelight. Carter was finding it suddenly very difficult to keep lying to her, to remain in his Texan role. Gradually, he allowed his drawl to slip away.

You never did explain why you picked me. You didn't see me at Armando's. You've never been there. I'm sure you don't even know where it is. So why me? I can't be that special."

He held his wineglass up so that the candle flame sparkled in it. Next to her face the crimson points of light made a beautiful contrast with the delicate smoothness of her complexion. "You're wrong there, Roberta," he said. "Very wrong." And as soon as he'd said it, he knew he'd spoken the truth.

They finished dinner, and after another glass of wine and some light conversation, mostly about life in the States, they moved to the couch. She put on some soft music, then came back to him.

They lay back, arm in arm, her eyes half-closed, her breasts rising and falling with her breathing. For a long time they listened to the music, luxuriating in the comfort of the moment.

She finally broke the silence.

"Why did you really come up to the office, Nick?"

"You don't believe me?"

"Not really," she said. "You came up there for something, saw me, and decided I was the means to your end. What was it you were looking for?"

There is no such thing as the perfect job. Every endeavor has its not-so-pleasant aspects. This was one of the worst. He hated lying to an innocent.

"What if I told you the truth—and it would make your position difficult?"

"Try me," she said languidly.

"What if it could make your life here . . . untenable?"

She opened her eyes and looked up into his. She reached up and drew him down to her. They kissed, deeply.

When they parted, there was a lot of color in her cheeks. "Try me," she said.

"I didn't follow you up to your office. You know that. In fact you came as a complete surprise to me . . . a pleasant surprise."

"You came up to see Mr. Ziegler?"

"I came up to find out whatever I could about him, and to . . . to make him nervous."

"I don't understand, Nick. Has Mr. Ziegler done something to you?"

"Someone tried to kill me several days ago in Iceland. Another tried up in Salto the day before yesterday. Both of them worked for your boss."

"But why?"

"Because I'm getting very close to uncovering something he's doing in Iceland. Something he wants to keep secret because it is illegal." Carter hesitated a moment, then smiled at her. "I thought I could charm the information out of you, but the reverse has happened."

She smiled and drew him down again. They kissed for a very long time. She combed back a lock of his dark hair with her fingertips. "You really mean that?" she asked, her voice very husky.

"Yes," he whispered, and he untied the drawstring at the neckline of her blouse. She wore no bra. Her breasts were small and firm, the nipples hard. He kissed them lightly, and a moan escaped from her lips.

Her hands and lips were all over him, and soon they slid slowly to the thick pile carpeting. They were nude, in each other's arms, making love with a barely restrained violence.

Afterward she lay in his arms, her eyes closed, a gentle smile on her lips. He sat above her, watching the candlelight dance on the perfect smoothness of her back, tracing its outline with his finger.

"What is it you're trying to find out, Nick?" she asked.

"What?"

"About Mr. Ziegler. What are you looking for?"

Carter had to bring his mind back to the present. "You said he's always busy. Doing what?" he asked lamely.

"Meetings. Telephone calls. Traveling. That sort of thing. There's always a lot of work in the mornings when I come in. Work that had to have been generated the previous evenings."

"Such as?"

"Inventory a lot of the time. Bills of lading, bills of transport, new numbers to put in the materials file."

"The president of a big concern handles that?"

"It's always been that way," she said.

"He's gathering up a new inventory, then. But what? And where's it coming from?"

She shook her head. "It's just numbers on a page to me, Nick. I don't know what the actual inventory is. I'm sorry. Do you think it's that important?"

"It might be."

"Once I remember sending a series of letters to a factory in Germany. I remember that specific incident because Mr. Ziegler seemed to be very worried about it."

"To Germany?"

"Yes, Mainz. It was something about a shortage of some items on a shipment."

"Where was all this shipped?"

"I don't know, Nick. It could have been anywhere. We have warehouses in sixteen different countries."

"Iceland?"

"No," she said. "Mostly in Europe, and here in South America."

"Here in Buenos Aires?"

"We have a lot of warehouses here."

"Where?" Nick asked. "Where specifically?"

"It depends upon what's being stored. I mean if it's paper goods, or hardware, or—"

"Something bulky, let's say," Nick interjected. "Something perhaps that might come in from Germany, and then would be immediately shipped out."

"Warehouse number four," she said without hesitation.

"What?"

"Number four. Avenida del Libertador. The Riacheulo District. It's the main clearinghouse for anything incoming or outgoing."

"Terrific," he said, sitting up. If Ziegler was supplying Iceland with anything—anything at all—it would probably go through this shipping point. It was worth a try.

Carter disengaged himself from Roberta and got up.

"You're not going out there now?"

He started getting dressed. "I have to find out what's going on there," he said.

She sat up. "But it's after one in the morning. And if they find you there, there's no telling what might happen."

Carter pulled her up to him and held her in his arms for a long moment. "I'm going to have to do this, but you're going to have to promise me something."

They parted, and she looked into his eyes but said nothing.

"I may have screwed things up for you at work. I don't want you going in until you hear from me. Do you understand?"

"No," she said, shaking her head.

"Your boss tried to kill me. Twice. Now he knows that you and I have spoken. He may know that we've had lunch, and that we've . . . been here together. Just stay here."

"All right," she said in a small voice.

He finished getting dressed, his weapons hidden in his jacket pockets.

"I get the terrible feeling that I'll never see you again. That I'm just going to have to hang around here in limbo for the rest of my life," Roberta said. Her eyes were glistening.

He kissed her. "I'll be back one way or the other," he said. "You can count on it."

They kissed again, and he left the apartment. In the

elevator on the way down to his car, he promised himself that when this thing was over, he would take her somewhere. Perhaps the Bahamas. Hawk would have to give him the time off.

Downstairs in the Audi he strapped on his weapons, then studied the car agency's city map. The Riachuelo District was on the city's far south side. When he had some idea where to go, he started the engine and left.

He stopped at his hotel to pick up a few items from his suitcase—a camera and a packet of tools— then he continued on to the docks.

When he arrived he found the banks of the Rio de la Plata shrouded in fog. He turned left off the main street, up a cobblestone lane, and then bumped along, his headlights narrowed to cones, looking for the proper warehouse.

The numbers, for some reason, did not run consecutively, and it was only by accident that he finally came upon number four. The building was very large and well lit. The main dockside doors were wide open, with a lot of activity coming and going.

A ship was being unloaded. And everyone seemed to be in one hell of a hurry.

Carter continued past the warehouse, finding a spot for his car a block beyond the building. He hurried back on foot to a point just down the dock from the warehouse where he could watch what was going on.

Men drove forklifts in and out of the warehouse as loads of cargo were lowered from the ship. The cargo was mostly very large crates, but occasionally there were bundles of large-diameter pipe—apparently plastic pipe of some sort.

As he continued to watch, a security guard with a vicious-looking German shepherd watchdog at his side and an automatic rifle—what appeared to be an AK-47—over his shoulder stepped into view in front of the doors. He nodded to one of the workmen, then walked to the other side of the building and disappeared around the corner.

Whatever was being unloaded must have been very important. They were taking no chances with its safety. Carter wondered if the armed guard was in any way a reaction to his visit to the company headquarters.

He slipped back into the shadows and, keeping low, raced across the narrow alleyway to a neighboring building.

The warehouse was dark, its service door at the side padlocked. It took him less than a minute to pick the lock and slip inside.

Even in the dark it wasn't hard to find the freight elevator and take it to the roof, but once he was outside he realized that the fog was thicker up here than at street level for some reason. The roof of number four appeared as nothing but a gray hulk lit from below. It was difficult to judge the exact distance from this roof to the other.

At the edge of the roof he looked across. It was fifteen feet, at least, to the roof of the next building. If he missed, it was at least fifty feet to the alley below. He'd end up as dog food for the German shepherd if he miscalculated.

Carter stepped back, counting off his paces until he was twenty yards away from the edge. Then, without the slightest hesitation, he raced toward the edge, putting everything he had into building up his speed.

There was no parapet on the roof, so one moment he was running and the next found him launched across the gap between the buildings.

His motion through the air seemed unreal in the dense fog; it seemed as if he were flying forever. But then the edge of the opposite building came up at his face, and he had just enough time to reach out with his arms to block his fall and hang on to the edge of the roof.

The impact nearly tore his arms from their sockets, but in the next instant he had heaved himself up onto the edge and lay there, his chest heaving.

The dog barked below, and seconds later Carter could hear the guard screaming at the animal to keep quiet.

He rolled over, got up, and moved silently to the nearest skylight. Below, in the warehouse, the crates were stacked nearly to the ceiling. He had to break one of the windowpanes in the skylight to get at the latch, but then it swung open easily, and he lowered himself inside atop the stack of crates.

He was near the rear of the warehouse. Most of the work being done now was toward the front. He flipped on his tiny penlight and examined the crate on which he was perched. Stenciled on the lid were the words FABRIZIERT IM DDR—Made in West Germany—giving Mainz as the point of origin. The logo was two lions holding up a shield with STEUBEN UND SOHNS lettered beneath it. He pulled out his miniature camera and took a photograph of the labeling, then let himself down crate by crate until he reached the floor at the rear of the building.

Wide aisles had been left between the tall stacks, and by keeping to the rear of the building, Carter could remain out of sight of the activity in the front.

His tiny camera was loaded with ultra-high-speed film, and as he worked his way past the stacks, he took photographs of the markings and numbers on the crates. Occasionally a piece of equipment was too large to be crated and instead was covered with plastic sheeting. He took photographs of these pieces of equipment as well.

At the end of one aisle he found a particularly large piece of gear covered in plastic. Careful to make as little noise as possible, he pulled back some of the plastic to get a better look. He'd ripped away a large section when he heard a low, menacing growl in the darkness behind him.

He spun around in time to catch no more than a blur as the dog charged him. He threw up his arm to protect his face as the dog hit, then went down under the force of the impact, the camera skating across the concrete floor.

The animal had been trained to go for the face and neck of its victim, and it was very strong and very quick.

He managed to shove the animal back far enough so that he got his left arm free. He pulled out his stiletto, and when the animal came at him again, he jabbed up into the beast's belly and sliced hard and to the left.

The animal whimpered in mortal pain, leaped away from

Carter, and ran around in tight circles snapping at its own
entrails.

Someone was shouting from the front of the warehouse,
and he could hear other dogs barking, and he scrambled to his
feet. The camera had evidently slid under one of the pallets,
but there was no time to search for it now.

He dashed down the nearest aisle, then through a gap in the
crates to the next aisle over, and halfway down that one until
he found a nest of cardboard boxes on the second tier up. He
hurried up the crates and shoved his way behind the
cardboard boxes, hidden from view from below.

He was covered with blood—the dog's as well as his own.
The animal had bitten his left hand, puncturing the skin and
tearing the flesh. It was very painful. He pulled out his
handkerchief and wrapped the wound, tightening the knot
with his teeth.

From the rear of his perch he could just see a section of the
area where the dog had attacked him. The animal lay dead. A
forklift came into view and stopped. Then two guards with
dogs hurried up. They all were armed with AK-47 Russian
assault rifles.

"He's probably still in the warehouse," the tallest of the
three men barked in German. He gave instructions to the
other two to spread out, and they started back along the aisle.

Carter glanced up the stack of boxes toward the skylights
in the ceiling. It was a long way up there, and he would be
exposed. There was no way in hell he'd get out the way he'd
gotten in.

He pulled out his Luger, checked the clip in the dim light,
and levered a round into the chamber. Before he left he was
going to have to retrieve the camera. It was the sole reason he
had risked coming here in the first place. Without it, he
would have all but wasted his time here tonight.

He eased himself down from his hiding place and hurried
down the aisle, keeping to the shadows, putting as much
distance as he could between himself and the guards with the
dogs.

Gradually he worked his way around so that he was on the

opposite side of the aisle where the camera lay. He could see the entire area clearly. The dog that had attacked him lay dead, sprawled against a crate. There was blood everywhere.

A dog suddenly began barking in the next aisle over, and Carter could hear the sounds of forklifts at the front still working.

He stepped out from behind the crate he had been watching from and started toward where he thought the camera might have slid when a second dog barked, this one much closer and directly behind him.

Carter spun around in time to see the animal charging at him from fifteen yards down the aisle. He leaped forward to the stack of crates and managed to pull himself halfway up when the animal had him by his left leg. He turned back, pointing Wilhelmina directly at the beast's head, about to pull the trigger, but then he stopped. Two men, both with AK-47s, stood looking at him.

"Hans! Back!" one of them snapped. The animal backed down, whining.

For just a moment Carter considered shooting it out with them, but then he decided against it. There was no way in hell he had a chance against their firepower.

He tossed his Luger down to the nearest guard, jumped down to the floor, and raised his hands.

"We'll take the knife you used to kill the other dog," the guard said in German.

Carter handed over Hugo, and the guard motioned toward the front of the building with the stiletto.

In front, the workmen were taking a break. They sat on boxes and machinery with their lunch pails open. They stopped and looked up when Carter and the guards appeared, then laughed and pointed. Some money changed hands.

"This way," one guard ordered, nudging Carter to the left with the barrel of the automatic.

They crossed the main entryway and went into the small front office equipped only with a couple of desks, a few swivel chairs, and a few file cabinets. One of the guards pulled out a chair and shoved Carter into it, while the other knocked softly at a rear door.

"*Kommen*," a rough voice commanded.

The guard opened the door and just stuck his head inside. "We have the spy, Herr General," he said.

The man in the back room came out. He was tall, completely bald, and wore a monocle in his right eye. It was Ziegler. There was no mistaking him. His thin, bloodless lips parted in a smile.

"Tie him to the chair," he snapped.

Quickly the guards produced some rope, and expertly bound Carter's arms and legs as well as his waist and chest.

"It is a long journey from Iceland to this place," Ziegler said in German, perching on the edge of one of the desks. "Who sent you?"

Carter just looked at the man, a slight smile on his face.

"You are going to die, Herr Carter. There is no question of that. However, how painful your death may or may not be is entirely up to you."

"Did you personally handle Lydia Coatsworth's death as well?" Carter asked. "You torture women too?"

"Break his fingers," Ziegler said nonchalantly to the guards. "Start with the pinky on his injured hand."

One of the guards roughly grabbed Carter's hand, but Ziegler held him back.

"Not so fast, Wilhelm. With care. Slowly, with care. We want Herr Carter to enjoy this."

The guard carefully began prying back the little finger on Carter's left hand, the pain shooting up his arm.

"Now," Ziegler said. "Who is it you work for? The CIA, perhaps?"

Carter held his silence, relaxing his body, letting the pain wash over him, through him, not fighting it.

The guard pulled the finger farther back, and the pain worsened. Carter could feel the sweat popping out on his forehead.

Ziegler shook his head sadly, then nodded toward the

guard, who pulled the finger the rest of the way back until it popped, the breaking bone sending a huge bolt of pain through the back of Carter's head . . . almost as if he had received a massive electric shock.

"There are nine fingers remaining. Then the toes. And if all else fails, there are interesting things to be done with your anus, or perhaps even your testicles." Ziegler chuckled.

The guard moved to Carter's ring finger.

"I'll tell you," Carter shouted. "Christ, it's not worth this."

The guard stopped. Ziegler just stared at him.

"Lydia Coatsworth was a close friend of mine. We . . . were lovers. She sent me a letter telling me she was in some kind of trouble. When she died I went up to see what happened."

The guard pulled Carter's Luger and the stiletto out of his jacket pocket, and handed them to Ziegler. "He was armed with these, Herr General."

Ziegler looked at them, then set the weapons on the desk. "Not CIA," he said thoughtfully. He looked at Carter. "How did you know about this warehouse?"

"Hauptmann told me before I killed him. He told me everything when I threatened to cut his eyes out and leave him there. He told me about you and the Odessa. About the operation up there as well as down here. About this place. About Steuben and Sons. The shipments from Mainz. Everything."

"He's lying, Herr General," one of the guards said. "Victor would never talk like that."

"Perhaps . . . perhaps not," Ziegler said. "*Every* man has his breaking point."

"I am a reporter with Amalgamated Press. In Washington, D.C.," Carter said. His entire hand and arm throbbed.

Ziegler looked at him thoughtfully.

"You can check on my credentials."

"Shall I break another finger, Herr General?" the guard asked. His breath smelled of onions.

"No," Ziegler said after a hesitation. "Tonight is the last

shipment in any event. It'll be on its way north by tomorrow.'' He smiled. ''Dispose of him. Down the elevator shaft.'' He picked up the Luger and stiletto, and handed them over to the guards. ''Put these back on his body.''

''Yes, sir,'' the guard said. He untied Carter while the other guard stood back, the AK-47 raised, and helped him out of the chair.

Outside, the workmen were finishing their meal. They watched as Carter and the guards headed toward the rear of the building. Carter walked slowly, regaining his strength and balance, making the guard crowd him.

A stairway against the back wall led to a second-floor balcony across from which was a freight elevator. One of the guards held the button, sending the car above the landing, but then he stopped it there and pulled the gate open on the gaping square hole.

''It goes down to the second basement. Forty feet, with steel pilings down there. Very unpleasant.''

Carter stood at the edge.

''You should have been more careful around this shaft,'' the guard said. The other one laughed.

At that moment Carter swung around, shoving the barrel of the gun away in one movement and spinning the guard around with the next, dropping him neatly into the elevator shaft.

The second guard was bringing his gun up as Carter leaped on him, smashing the man's throat with a karate chop. The guard went down, his rifle clattering on the balcony floor.

There was no time to waste, Carter thought. He recovered his stiletto and Luger from the unconscious but still breathing guard, then hurried down the stairs, and up the aisles and rows to where the dead dog still lay.

Using his tiny penlight, it took him only a minute or two to find where the camera had slid beneath one of the pallets. Quickly he pulled back the plastic cover on a big piece of machinery, took several more photographs, then pocketed the camera.

He had gotten what he had come for and more. This

equipment was bound for Iceland tomorrow. The connection between Ziegler and what was happening up there was very clear now.

There was a commotion up on the balcony. Someone shouted something from above, and a siren sounded. They had discovered the guard.

He pulled out his Luger and raced toward the far corner of the large warehouse, ducking down aisles and up rows, keeping low and moving as fast as he could.

More dogs were barking from behind him now, and he could hear men shouting even over the howl of the siren.

The service door at the rear of the building was latched from inside. It took him a moment or two to fumble with the locking bar, but then he had it open and he was outside.

A half-dozen men, all of them armed, came around the corner from the front, cutting off any chances he had of making it to where he had parked his car.

Instead, he ducked around the back of the building and raced around to the other side, then went back to the front of the building.

At the corner he peered around. There were several men standing in the big doorway, their backs to him. Straight across from where he stood, the dock was only twenty yards wide, dropping off beside the ship to the water.

He holstered his Luger, took a deep breath and let it out slowly, then bolted from the corner of the building and ran directly across the dock.

He was nearly to the water when someone behind him shouted, ''It's him!'' But he was over the edge as the first shots were fired.

The water was fifteen feet below the dock, and he hit cleanly, feet first, the cold waters of the Rio de la Plata washing over his head.

He came up swimming, just making it around the bow of the ship before a fusillade of shots sounded from above him on the dock.

He dove deeply this time, swimming away from the ship at

right angles. When he came up, the firing was still going on, and there were more sirens sounding in the distance, but it was all behind him.

He struck out across the docks, finally coming to a small diesel-powered fishing boat tied to a dilapidated pier. He climbed up over the side, lay on top of the stinking nets for a few moments to catch his breath, then hot-wired the ignition and swung the boat out into the open water, heading north-west, toward Montevideo.

SEVEN

The economic information officer to the U.S. envoy in Montevideo felt a buzz of excitement as he ran up the stairs from the basement parking lot under the embassy. He hadn't had a thrill like this since the Cuban Revolution.

Just half an hour ago, when he had come home late from work, had parked his car, and had started up the back walk to his apartment, the intelligence officer had leaped like an apparition out of the garbage dumpster brandishing a gun.

"I don't want to hurt you," the man had said.

The information officer, whose name was Putnam, had worked for the CIA some years ago, and he knew better than to argue with an apparently overwrought man with a gun. They went back to Putnam's car, got in, the man on the floor in the back, and Putnam did as he was told.

As they drove back into town, the man explained what he wanted Putnam to do for him. He had a packet of film, he said, that had to be sent out in the diplomatic pouch immediately. There would be some phone calls he would have to make, but they could wait until Putnam was absolutely sure the embassy was essentially cleared for the night.

In the meantime he needed a first-aid kit, and he would wait in the car while Putnam went up and got it from the dispensary.

"Your name is Robert Putnam," the man said. He gave

Putnam a number to call in Washington, D.C., and an index. "Before you do anything, Putnam, check that out."

Putnam gained the top landing of the stairs and found the first floor of the embassy deserted, as was usual at this time of night. Upstairs in communications there would be the duty officers, but nothing moved down here except the guards.

The guard station was at the front of the building, and the marine on duty looked up as Putnam strode by. But he said nothing.

Back in the dispensary, Putnam pulled out a first-aid kit, then picked up the telephone, rang up to communications, and had them place the call to Washington. It only took a minute or two, and the phone rang only once before it was answered with the number by a woman.

Putnam gave the index word and number, and the woman described Carter, got the details of who was calling, from where, and the circumstances, then asked Putnam to help in any way he could. She gave a Washington address for the film.

After the call, he went up to communications, leaving the first-aid kit out in the corridor, and handed the film cartridges to the OD, along with the Washington address. "These get sent in the sack first thing in the morning."

"Yes, sir," the young OD said. "But there is one out tonight at midnight."

"That's even better. Get it in that one then, please."

"Yes, sir."

Back out in the corridor, Putnam grabbed the first-aid kit and hurried back down to the parking garage. The woman on the phone had identified the man as Nick Carter. He was lying in the back seat. Putnam helped him out of the car and to the elevator.

"Nearly everyone is gone, sir," he said. "I can get you up to my office without the marines seeing us."

"I may have to stay awhile," Carter said; his tongue seemed thick. "I'll need something to eat and drink."

"Yes, sir," Putnam said. This was great.

They got up to the third floor without incident, and Putnam helped Carter down the corridor and into his office, where he locked the door before he flipped on the light.

It was a tiny cubicle, but it had a small couch along one wall. He settled Carter back on the couch, doused his hand in disinfectant after pulling off the blood-encrusted handkerchief, put a splint on the badly broken finger, and finally bandaged the bites.

He poured Carter a drink of brandy from the bottle in his desk, lit him a cigarette, then sat back and watched him.

"You said you wanted to make some phone calls?" Putnam asked when it seemed as if Carter was beginning to recover.

"Right. Have you sent off my film?"

"It'll leave at midnight tonight. Should be in Washington by late morning. Your . . . office knows it's coming."

"Do they know where I am?"

"Yes, sir."

Carter sat back with his cigarette, seemed to think a moment, then looked up. He seemed very determined.

"Are you game to help me a bit more, Putnam?" he asked.

"Yes, sir. Anything you say."

"Get me that Washington number again, then take a walk for about five minutes."

"Yes, sir," Putnam said. He got communications again and placed the call. When it started to ring, he handed the phone across and left the office.

The phone was answered immediately.

"Carter, blue bird seven-three-zero."

The line went dead. Two minutes later David Hawk's voice came on. "I just got word you were in Montevideo. Are you all right?"

"A little shaken up. I've sent up some film. You should have it in the morning." Quickly and succinctly Carter told Hawk everything that had happened.

Hawk thought about it for a moment. "Ziegler knows you're after him, and he knows you're obviously not a newsman. It'll make him nervous. Maybe he'll make a mistake or two."

"My thoughts exactly, sir."

"Did you get a good look at the equipment you were photographing?"

"Yes, sir."

"Hang on—I'll put Cairnes on and maybe he can give us some ideas." Moments later the connection was made. Hawk was speaking to the chief of AXE's technical section. "Carter is on the line. He's taken a look at some equipment. See if you can make head or tail of it."

"Go ahead, N3," Cairnes's nasal voice said.

Carter explained in detail everything he had seen in the warehouse.

"A nuclear reactor or reactors, I'd guess," Cairnes said. "The big one was probably a waste water eliminator, standard for a breeder reactor. Steuben and Sons are the biggest manufacturers of that kind of equipment. But . . ."

"But what, Bill?" Hawk asked.

"That equipment could be for other purposes as well. Steam movement. Hot water transport. Even sewage disposal. Hell, there's no real way of telling without more information."

"Nick?" Hawk asked.

"I can leave for Mainz by morning. I'll have to get my things from Buenos Aires. Juan can do that for me. The embassy here can arrange my travel."

Someone knocked at the door, and Putnam stuck his head in. Carter waved him in.

"I have to ring off now, sir."

"Keep in touch," Hawk said. "I'll have our people in Bonn keep an eye out for you."

"Yes, sir," Carter said, and he hung up.

Putnam had brought a couple of sandwiches and a few beers with him. "The commissary wasn't locked, and you said you were hungry."

Carter took one of the sandwiches and a beer. "I'm beginning to like you, Putnam . . . a lot."

Putnam beamed.

"We have a lot of things to get done tonight," Carter said. "I hope you're used to staying up all night."

"I can manage, sir. Just name it."

"First, I'll need to have my things brought up from the Sheraton in Buenos Aires. Tonight. Next I'm going to have to contact a man by the name of Juan Mendoza, who'll have to take a message to a friend for me. Then I'll need a doctor to set this finger, and I'll need to speak with the chargé d'affaires for travel arrangements."

"Back to the States, sir?"

"No," Carter said.

Twenty-four hours later, Carter sat on a bench at the north end of Messerschmidt Park in Mainz, Germany, staring at the Steuben and Sons facility just across the street.

Mainz had been one of the principal Allied bombing targets during the war because of the Krupp munition works that had been located here. From the looks of it, Steuben and Sons had also been a part of that targeted industrial complex. A two-story-high wall of masonry still surrounded the plant to protect it from flash fires ignited by bombs in the city. The pads that had once held antiaircraft guns were still visible on the turrets at the corners of the walls.

Carter had already made a complete circuit of the factory's perimeter and had found the enclosure complete. The only way in or out was by the front or rear gates, or a single metal door. And the back gates seemed unused. Debris had been piled up over the top on the inside.

He crushed his cigarette on the sidewalk, then went back to his rented car parked around the corner from the main entrance. It was 2:10 in the afternoon. He pulled up near the corner so that he could see the main gate, then shut off the ignition and lit another cigarette.

At three the shift changed. A river of people streamed out one side of the front gate, while the evening shift streamed in. Most of the evening crew came by trollies that stopped at the corner, but a good number drove, filing the parking spaces along the park for several blocks on either side of the plant.

By 3:20 the streets were deserted again, and Carter was about to go back to his hotel to wait until dark, when a battered Volkswagen rounded the corner and sped up the street in his direction. A man dressed in workmen's clothes was driving. The car stopped short in the next block, and the driver tried to wedge into a parking space, but it was too small, and he continued on, turning the next corner.

He was circling. And he was late for work.

Carter jumped out of his car as the VW emerged on the far side of the park and disappeared again behind a line of brick houses. When it did not appear at the next street, Carter sprinted through the park, across a deserted playground, and over a ten-foot-tall wire-mesh fence. This put him at the rear of the brick houses, and when he made it to the front he found the car hastily jammed between a microbus and another VW. The driver was rummaging for something in the back seat.

Carter climbed in on the passenger side, his Luger drawn. The man's eyes widened.

"Is this a robbery?" he stammered. "I have nothing. I am late for work."

"Drive," Carter ordered in German. He raised the gun, and the man started the car, eased out of the parking place, and drove down the street.

There were too many houses there. Too many possibilities for someone to see what was going on and report it to the police.

Carter directed the frightened man to drive into the park and to stop behind the restroom building. There were only a few people in the park, all of them too far away to see what was happening. Carter brought the man into the empty men's room, where he made him take off his clothes. They switched clothes, then Carter bound and gagged the hapless worker in a stall.

The workman might have to stay there for a few hours, Carter decided, but he'd be okay.

Back at the man's VW, Carter clipped on the workman's ID badge, then he drove back out of the park and found a spot for the car two blocks away from his own car. He put on the workman's hard hat, grabbed his lunch pail, and headed up the street. At his own car he pulled out his camera and stuffed it in his pocket, then continued around the corner to the front gate.

He was Dieter Mueller from nearby Wertheim. Thirty-three years old, dark hair like Carter, and only a bit larger and heavier, so the clothes looked all right. Unless the gate man looked closely at the employee badge, or personally knew Mueller, there would be no problem.

The guard at the gate was busy talking on the phone. From his hip hung a huge, American-made, military .45 automatic. Carter hurried by, doing his best to appear worried about being late, and the guard glared at him, presumably for the same reason. But he said and did nothing, and Carter was inside.

Across the driveway, which split to the right toward the offices, Carter went left into the main factory building through a door marked Employees Only. He followed the safety notices down the narrow corridor and punched in at the time clock, finding Mueller's card with no problem. At least the man would get paid for today.

Inside the main workshop, it was incredibly noisy. Hydraulic hammers smacked parts out of thick sheet steel and sent them cooling down long assembly-line chains.

He hurried through the forming room and out on the other side into the factory yard. He was going to have to find out where they assembled the type of equipment he had seen on the docks in Buenos Aires. More photos were needed for a positive identification.

Outside, piles of material had been laid in neat rows with narrow aisles between them. Carter stood in the midle of one of the aisles trying to decide which way to try next, when a hoarse toot sounded behind him. He jumped just in time to avoid being run down by a forklift loaded with machine parts.

"Vorsicht, Jungen!" shouted a hard-boiled old man at the wheel, as he pulled up to a halt.

"Where is the assembly plant?" Carter shouted.

The old man turned, dropped his load expertly in its place, and backed up next to Carter. "New here . . . Mueller?" he asked, peering at the ID badge.

Carter nodded.

"Get on! I'm heading over there now."

Carter got a foothold, and they took off through the forest of machine parts, some piles of plastic piping, and several very large castings. The old man was an expert at getting around tight places, and within minutes they were rolling into a busy, brightly lit section of the factory, filled with huge hulks of machinery. The brilliant pinpoint lights of welding torches shone everywhere. Along the ceiling high overhead, a massive crane moved down the room. Dangling from the crane's cable was an enormous hollowed-out half-cylinder; Carter recognized it as the outer casting of the pump he was looking for. They were building another.

He shouted his thanks to the old man and jumped off the forklift, which continued across the assembly plant and out the other side. The pump casting overhead disappeared behind a barrier of corrugated iron that cordoned off one section of the work area. Along the barrier the stenciled word VER-BOTEN appeared every few feet. The only gap in the barrier was the ceiling-high door through which the crane had passed. Beside the opening was a security guard, nodding at each man who came or went from inside. Personal recognition, Carter thought with a sinking feeling.

It would take some maneuvering to get around the guard, but he had come this far unchallenged; he wasn't going to stop this close to his goal. Yet he couldn't afford to have the alarm raised. He'd need time to take his photographs and then to get out with the film. He was going to have to be very careful.

He turned and started down the aisle in the opposite direction when he saw three men inspecting the spot welds on a section of pipe. One wore work clothes and the white hard hat Carter assumed was a foreman's. The second was in a business suit, and between them stood a taller man wearing a light jacket and slacks, and a white hard hat. He half turned, the harsh fluorescent light glinting off a lens over one eye.

Ziegler.

Carter retreated, walking hastily across the work area, cursing his luck. Ziegler had lost him in Buenos Aires, and he had run here to Germany to make sure nothing interfered with the work he had ordered. Goddamnit! He was the one man in Germany at this moment who could recognize him.

He hurried past an extruding machine, shooting out long sections of plastic piping, and past some other machinery whose purpose he could only guess at.

Overhead, the crane's empty cables sailed by. He followed the arc of their flight and saw the second half of the pump casting waiting by the huge outer doors. Two men stood in front of it, waiting.

He stepped up his pace, overtaking the cables, but not moving so fast as to attract any attention. Then he slipped around the huge pump casting to the inside, between it and the wall.

The huge hulk was shaped more or less like a teapot with three spouts: lower, middle, and upper. He tossed his lunch pail aside, grabbed the lip of the lower spout, and hoisted himself inside, just pulling his feet in as the cable's hook clanged noisily on the outer surface of the casting.

In a few minutes the cables were secured, and Carter felt the weightless surge as the casting swept into the air.

A panorama of the floor passed by the angle of his view

from the spout as the massive piece of metal swung lazily on the chain. A minute later he could see the iron barrier, and the casting began to descend.

The pump hit the floor with a jolt, thrusting Carter deeper into the spout, almost into the main body. Then someone was directly below him as the cables were unhooked. They were saying something, the words coming only indistinctly to him where he lay.

After a few minutes the voices faded, and there were only the factory noises for an hour or two after that. At first he had feared that the two parts would be assembled immediately, and he would be discovered. But now he wondered how long it would be before he could get out of there.

As if on cue, a loud buzzer sounded, and gradually machines stopped, lunch pails rattled, and he could hear the men tromping away from the shop. Dinner break, he guessed, and in a few minutes the factory was silent.

Carter inched his way into the tank, and when he was clear of the spout, he stood up. A guard, seated by the door, was just visible from around the edge of the pump casting. The man was reading a magazine as he ate his dinner.

Carter took out his camera and, careful to make absolutely no noise, took several photographs of the pump casting he was standing inside of and of its mate on the other side of the shop floor.

He stepped out of the casting and, keeping it between himself and the guard, moved through the shop area, snapping photographs of the equipment and gears that evidently were to be installed inside the castings.

When he was finished, he stuffed the camera back in his pocket and went around the far side of the casting in which he had ridden.

The guard was still engrossed in his magazine. Carter picked up a large chunk of slag from the floor and threw it across the large shop. It clattered off the side of the twin casting.

The guard jumped to his feet, the magazine falling to the

floor. *"Was ist?"* he shouted. He took a couple of steps forward, then hurried across to the other casting.

When he was around the opposite side, Carter hurried out into the main shop, then sprinted across toward the main doors leading outside. Suddenly in the wide doorway a knot of men appeared. At the forefront was the steelworker whose clothing he had stolen. He looked angry.

"Damn," Carter swore. He wheeled a hundred and eighty degrees and headed back toward the iron barrier. Just then the guard came out.

"Here, what are you doing?" the guard shouted, his hand on the butt of his automatic.

"They asked me to come fetch you, sir," Carter said, pointing to the men across the factory.

The guard looked uncertainly that way.

"You'd better hurry, sir. They're mad."

"Verdammt," the guard swore, and he headed across the factory as Carter sprinted in the opposite direction to the left of the iron barrier.

At the rear of the building he went through a set of swinging doors into a packaging area. Three men in carpenter's aprons looked up from their dinners as Carter shot past.

Somewhere behind him an alarm bell sounded. Up ahead loomed the loading dock where flatbed rail cars stood waiting to haul the finished equipment to Bremen for shipment west. Powerful cranes stood by to lift the heavier pieces onto the cars while men with thick chains would batten them down.

The men out here were eating as well, but some of them stood up and were looking past him.

"What are all the alarms about?" one of them asked as Carter emerged.

"I don't know," Carter shouted, passing behind the car. "They don't tell me anything."

On the other side of the track was a grassy field that ran a hundred yards out to a series of old storage sheds and buildings adjacent to the perimeter wall.

He headed across the field at a fast trot as someone shouted something at him from behind. He ignored it but picked up his speed.

A shot was fired, and he began zigzagging across the field, keeping low as more shots were fired.

Halfway across the field he pulled out his Luger, rolled to the left, then scrambled up on one knee and squeezed off four shots in rapid succession. Two of the guards went down, and for a moment, at least, the firing stopped.

He jumped up and made it the rest of the way to the storage sheds. He ducked behind them, then went inside the larger one.

The oblong of dim twilight from the doorway revealed piles of old motors, stacks of pipe, and other old equipment rusting away.

He closed the door and started down the length of the shed, whose rear wall was formed by the brick of the perimeter wall, looking for a break, perhaps a wooden door or some weak spot.

Light appeared behind him as the door swung open again and a shot sounded, the bullet ricocheting off a metal object to his left.

He hurried deeper into the darkness as other shots were fired, then someone switched on a flashlight. The guards were framed for easy targets in the doorway, but he had not come here to kill anyone. He had come to get information. He had it, and now he merely wanted to get free.

Another shot rang out from behind. They were firing at random, not able to see anything because of the darkness.

Carter came to the metal door set into the thick outer wall. A rusted, ancient padlock held it closed.

He checked his Luger. There were only five shots left. Carefully he aimed to the left of the doorway behind him—he was certain there were no guards standing there—and squeezed off three shots. Someone shouted, and they all took cover.

He turned, stood back, and fired two quick shots at the lock, the second one springing the rusted mechanism.

He holstered the gun and put his shoulder to the door, the ancient hinges giving way very slowly, until he had the door open about a foot, just enough to squeeze out.

Several more shots were fired toward him, these much closer, but by then he was outside and running down the street.

His first thought was the worker's Volkswagen, but the man had been with the guards; they'd have the car staked out. So he headed in a dead run around the corner toward his own car.

Another shot rang out behind him from the metal door through which he had just emerged. Damnit, he hadn't thought they'd shoot at him out here, on a public street.

Down the street a garbage truck turned the corner, the driver obviously in a hurry. The big truck tipped to the side under the strain of the acceleration.

Carter sprinted down the opposite curb as a car passed, and then he was behind the rapidly accelerating garbage truck. He grabbed the handrails at the back and swung aboard, keeping well to the outside so the guards pursuing him would not have a clear shot.

The truck lumbered around the corner, and Carter jumped off as it passed his car. He had his keys out and was racing around to the driver's side when two vans pulled up, each disgorging a half-dozen armed men. He pulled up short. The odds had just gone through the ceiling.

He raised his hands as Ziegler got out of the lead van and came toward him. The bald man did not look happy.

EIGHT

The tires crunched over what could only be crushed stone. And the air, Carter realized, was much too sweet for a city. They had to be outside in the country somewhere.

The car turned left and began ascending a steep hill punctuated with tight curves. When they hit a level spot, they stopped.

The two men in the front got out, and the driver opened the rear door. "Out!" he shouted in German. He reached in and grabbed Carter by the arm and pulled him off the back floor of the car.

The air was cool here, laced with a pine scent. The driver and the other man guided the blindfolded Carter across a grassy area, and then they started up a steep set of stairs. Carter stumbled purposely on the first step, falling to his knees.

"*Scheisse!*" the driver muttered in disgust. He cut through the cloth blindfold and pulled it away. Light flooded Carter's eyes, blinding him for a moment. He turned his head away until his vision began to return to normal and he was able to see the outlines of the mountains, the sun sparkling off the snow at the higher elevations. August. Still snow. They had to be many miles from Mainz.

"*Raus!*" the driver snarled, and they started up again.

High above, a small chalet was set into the face of the cliff.

• • •

121

"Kirschwasser?" Ziegler asked, opening a bottle. Carter stared sullenly into the crackling fire. The general poured himself a drink, then came back to where Carter was seated. The driver and the other one stood by the door. They seemed bored.

"Do you prefer German, or would you rather speak in English?" Ziegler asked, taking a seat across from Carter.

Carter held his silence. If he could get the man angry, he might make a mistake.

"German, then," the man said. "Apparently you are fluent with the language, whereas my English . . . well, I have been lax over the years." Ziegler took a sip of his drink. He seemed expansive. "The last time we talked, you represented yourself as a reporter. We checked with Amalgamated Press and found, of course, that you are on the payroll. But I think you are more than a mere reporter. Your facility with weapons suggests you have had training."

Carter looked nonchalantly out the large plate glass window which afforded a spectacular view of the mountains.

"I get quite cross when I am ignored, Herr Carter," Ziegler said. There was a slight edge to his voice.

"Untie my hands," Carter said, looking at him.

"Very well." Ziegler motioned for the men at the door. The driver came over and cut the bonds holding Carter's wrists. Carter brought his hands around in front of him and rubbed his wrists to restore the circulation. His fingers were numb.

"I'll have that drink now," he said.

"A glass for Herr Carter," Ziegler told his driver.

The man went to the bar, poured a drink, and brought it over. His face was devoid of expression, his eyes hooded.

Carter sipped thoughtfully. It tasted harsh yet bracing. If there were any drugs hidden in the drink, he couldn't detect the taste. "Quite a setup here, Herr General," Carter said. "Your Berghof?"

"You might say so," Ziegler said. "But that was another war in another time. We are here and now. And a project of mine is being seriously imperiled by your meddling.''

"Sorry about that—" Carter started to quip, but Ziegler cut him off.

"I will find out how much you know about my personal business and for whom you are working.''

"I have nine more fingers," Carter said, studying his bandaged hand. "Care to try for two out of ten?''

Ziegler smiled. It was the last expression Carter would have expected from the man, and it gave him a chill. "There are other methods," he said. He looked up at his men still at the door. "Bring her in.''

"Her?" Carter asked. He had a sick feeling in the pit of his stomach.

The driver stepped out of the room. Ziegler got up and went over to the fireplace where he took a poker from the stand and wedged it among the glowing coals.

"Ziegler . . . you bastard," Carter said. The other man by the door had pulled out his gun. He was staring at Carter. The slightest move and it would be all over.

The driver returned a moment or two later, pushing Roberta Redgrave in front of him. She had obviously been roughed up.

Carter started to rise, but he was looking into the very large barrel of a .44 magnum. He slumped back.

"Spare us any emotional displays," Ziegler said without looking around. He picked up a wooden bellows and began fanning the coals around the poker, which he had jammed between two logs.

Roberta seemed dazed. Her hair was matted with sweat. Carter guessed she had been drugged. Her skin was clear and unbruised, and her clothing, while wrinkled, didn't seem torn or soiled, but she had a look about her that told him she had been psychologically abused.

"You may be interested to know that your friend is an operative with the BND," Ziegler said. "The *Bundesnach-richtendienst.*" He kept pumping the bellows, the coals around the poker white hot now.

Carter's stomach flopped. Roberta an operative with the West German secret intelligence service. Was that why she had allowed him to approach her so easily? If it were true, she was good . . . very good indeed.

"Roberta?" he called out.

She didn't look up.

"She's in no condition to talk at the moment," Ziegler said, chuckling. "Although I'm sure we'll hear a great deal from her in a moment or two." He took out the poker and examined it. The first six inches of the thing glowed a bright red. "Sit the bitch down," Ziegler said, turning around.

The guard by the door pulled a chair out from around the coffee table, and the driver shoved Roberta down into it.

"Wait a moment," Carter said. They all turned to him except for Roberta, who stared down at her knees. When he spoke again, he made his voice sound strained, as if he were very frightened and totally intimidated by Ziegler and his methods. It was his only hope, at least for the moment.

"I'll tell you whatever you want to know. Just don't hurt her."

"I was right about you, after all. You *are* a sentimentalist," Ziegler said. He jammed the poker back into the fireplace and sat down.

"I am a trained intelligence officer," Carter said. "You were right. You had me pegged . . . although I don't know how."

"Who do you work for?"

"The government . . . the U.S. government, that is. But you have to believe me when I tell you that I'm here in no official capacity. I'm on leave."

"Interesting," Ziegler said. "Then why exactly is it you are here?"

"I've come to find out why Dr. Coatsworth was killed. She was a friend."

Ziegler took a cigarette from a silver case, then pushed the case back into his shirt pocket. "You certainly must think that I'm a fool," he said. He got up, went over to the fireplace, got the poker, and when he turned back he was smiling.

Carter could feel the sweat beginning to form on his chest.

Ziegler held out the poker, and the driver came across and took it from him. The other man trained his pistol on Carter.

"You don't have to do anything so crude," Carter said.

The driver brought the poker behind Roberta's chair. The son of a bitch was looking forward to it.

"I'm the only one who knows of the Odessa connection," Carter said. "I swear it. Hurting her won't change that."

Ziegler chuckled and nodded. The driver delicately touched the tip of the red-hot poker to the back of Roberta's neck, just below her ear. She screamed and jerked forward, falling facedown on the carpeted floor.

The stench of singed hair and burned flesh was strong in the air.

"You son of a bitch! You bastard!" Carter shouted in English. "Kill her and you'll have to kill me, and then you *will* be screwed, Herr General!"

The driver had gone around to the front of the chair, where he knelt down beside Roberta who lay there moaning.

Ziegler motioned for the man to hold up. "I will be screwed. Curious. Whatever do you mean by that, Herr Carter?"

"The nuclear power plant you're building in Iceland. You're diverting steam from Reykjavik to panic the Althing. You're bribing Josepsson and others. Lydia found out about it."

Ziegler looked at his driver. "There isn't much else we can do with either of them. Kill them both. We'll see who comes looking for them." He started to turn away, but then he looked back. "Make it look like an accident."

"*Jawohl, mein Herr,*" the driver said with obvious relish.

"But be careful, for God's sake," Ziegler said, looking at Carter. "This one is dangerous, I think."

The driver yanked Roberta to her feet after he put the poker back in its rack. She seemed only vaguely aware of what was going on. The other man tied Carter's hands behind his back, then jerked him to his feet.

Together the four of them went back outside, then down the long stairs to the parking area. There were several cars and a couple of small trucks parked there.

They went directly to a BMW sedan on top of which were a pair of skis in a rack. The guard shoved Roberta in the passenger side in the front, and Carter was shoved in the back. The driver and guard got in, and they pulled out of the parking lot and headed down the very steep road toward the base of the mountain. One side of the road was a sheer rock cliff that rose hundreds of feet above them. On the other side was a drop of at least a thousand feet to a rock-strewn ravine.

The car was no doubt registered to Hemispheric Technologies, and when the accident was "discovered," they'd claim he was an employee on holiday. Eventually Hawk and the West German government would figure out what really happened, but by that time Ziegler would have erased any personal connection with the incident.

When the guard had hurriedly tied his hands, Carter had flexed his wrist muscles; now he relaxed them, and the knots loosened slightly. As they had walked down the steep road, he worked at the bindings.

"Where are you taking us?" he asked the guard seated next to him. He had to distract the man.

The guard just looked at him and smiled. "A very short trip, *mein Herr*. You'll see." He laughed.

The thin nylon line was slipping.

"It's a shame," Carter said. "She's such a pretty girl."

The driver looked at him in the rearview mirror.

"What's a shame?" the guard in the back seat asked.

Carter shrugged. "She's a pretty girl. Helpless. You're going to kill us anyway . . ."

His guard's eyes narrowed. "What do you get out of this?"

"A cigarette, that's all," Carter said, a tremor in his voice. "I know what you're up to. Maybe a drink. And then at the end you can knock me out."

The driver laughed out loud at the same moment the bonds came loose on Carter's wrists.

"You're going to let the opportunity pass you by?" Carter said disdainfully.

His guard sat forward, reached over the front seat, and pulled Roberta's coat open.

"What the hell . . ." the driver said.

"Shut your mouth, Karl," the guard snapped. He ripped Roberta's blouse open and yanked her bra apart, freeing her lovely breasts.

They had taken Carter's Luger and stiletto, but they hadn't found Pierre, the tiny gas bomb.

The guard was laughing lustily as he fondled Roberta's breasts. Unnoticed, Carter managed to reach around to unzip his own trousers, reach inside, and withdraw the gas bomb, then shove his hands back behind him just as the guard turned to look at him.

"Tell me, was she a great piece of ass?" the guard sneered.

Carter almost killed him then and there, but he held back. "You can find that out for yourself."

"Pull over, Karl," the guard said.

"Son of a bitch," the driver snapped. "There's no place here." He glanced over at Roberta's exposed breasts. "About a mile. Near the hairpin turn. I'll stop there."

Of all the weapons in his arsenal, Carter liked the gas bomb the least. The first whiff knocked one unconscious, and a few seconds after exposure, respiration ceased altogether. A few seconds was precious little time to prevent the wrong people from dying.

Another mile of twists and turns, and they came upon a large patch of ice in the shadow of the mountain. It extended a quarter mile to where the road curved in front of a scenic overlook. It would have been a perilous stretch of highway in any event, but the ice made it a certain deathtrap for the unwary.

The driver slowed almost to a crawl, and they still slid slowly to the bottom of the hill, the bumper of the car just nudging the low stone fence at the precipice.

Far below, a mountain stream punished itself against the rocks, looking like little more than a thin, silver ribbon tangled at the bottom of a canyon. A car could lie down there for days without being discovered.

"Here?" the guard in the back seat panted. He was pawing Roberta's breasts.

The driver seemed frightened. He wrenched the gear lever in reverse, turned around, and headed back up the hill.

"You gotta stop, Karl! *Gott in Himmel!*" the guard slobbered. He was getting worked up.

Carter slipped his thumbnail into the gas bomb's trigger. Cyatelene gas—a cyanide derivative—began pouring through the tiny jets in the bomb's perimeter, filling the car with billows of smoke. The guard next to Carter started to turn around to reach for his gun, but he promptly dropped it and fell unconscious against the far window.

The driver started to roll down his window, but then he too slumped forward, and the car slowed, then stopped, and finally rolled backward at an angle across the road and down into a shallow ditch.

Roberta was out almost immediately, and the race began to get her outside before she took in too much.

Carter sprang forward, still holding his breath, unlatched her door, shoved it open, and pushed her outside as the car bumped to a halt.

He opened the rear door, his own perceptions beginning to become distorted, and fell outside, his legs rubbery. He'd held his breath, but the gas was affecting him anyway. Burnt almonds . . . it was all he could smell. For a split second he could not remember what it was he was supposed to be doing.

Then, summoning every ounce of strength and concentration he had, he pulled himself up toward where Roberta lay half in and half out of the car.

All he wanted to do was lie there and sleep. His muscles felt like lead. But he began to remember there was no time, and he managed to get up and stumble to Roberta's inert form.

He dragged her clear, then tried to pick her up, but it was hopeless. His muscles were too weak. He stumbled, dropped her, and ended up dragging her to the shoulder of the road, where he crouched over her prostrate body, panting. After several seconds the sharp, cold mountain air cleared his head, and his presence of mind returned. He took her pulse. It was dangerously weak.

Quickly he tilted her head back, pinched her nose, and started blowing air into her lungs. He kept it up for almost five minutes, but nothing seemed to be happening. God, he didn't want to lose her. Not like this.

He checked her pulse again. He felt nothing.

Frantically he put the heels of his hands together and began a rhythmic heart massage, her chest very small and delicate, her breasts tiny, the nipples rigid with the cold.

Her chest heaved after a few minutes, and her entire body shuddered as if an electrical current had run through it.

He continued to work feverishly, heedless of his own problems because of the gas. After a while the color began to come back to her cheeks, then her eyelids fluttered and opened.

"Nick," she breathed.

"Don't talk." He pulled off his thick workshirt, bundled it up, and placed it under her head. Then he got up and walked unsteadily back to the car.

After thirty seconds cyatelene gas combines with the oxygen in the air to form dicyateloxide, a harmless compound, But before its thirty seconds of potent life expired, Carter's bomb had taken its toll. The side of the driver's face lay against the steering wheel, his eyes bulging, his blackened tongue swelling out of his mouth. The guard in the back had fared no better.

He pulled the bodies out one at a time and dragged them off the road behind a jumble of rocks. Then he scuffed his tracks in the snow and went back to where Roberta lay on the gravel.

"How do you feel?" he asked.

"Woozy."

He helped her to her feet, and with an arm around her waist

he helped her to the car. He climbed in behind the wheel and started the engine.

"Are you going back?" Roberta asked.

Carter nodded, put the car in gear, made a careful U-turn, and headed back up the mountain.

Rivulets of melting snow were cutting channels in the gravel when they pulled into the parking lot below the mountain house. One of the cars that had been parked here earlier—the tan Mercedes—was missing.

"He's gone," Roberta said.

"Maybe not. But I'm going to check one way or the other."

"You don't even have a weapon," she said.

Beside them on the seat was the driver's weapon. An American military .45 automatic. "This'll do," he said. "You wait here. If you hear shooting, listen for the last shot, then count to ten. If you don't hear another, take off. Understand?"

She nodded.

His strategy was simple. The chalet was a modernistic affair with large plate glass windows in the front that looked down on the valley. In back, smaller windows opened onto a solid rock face. These were the bedroom windows, he figured. They'd be empty now, providing him easy access.

He climbed up the back way, working his way around the side of the house to the rear windows, which were set a few feet off the rock base and only a few feet away from the face of the cliff on which the house was perched.

Curtains were drawn over three of the windows, but the fourth was open, and he could see that the room inside was a bedroom.

The window was unlocked, and within a few seconds Carter stood in the middle of the bedroom, holding his breath as he listened to the sounds of the house. But there was nothing. In fact, he thought, the house was too quiet, as if everything had been shut down.

He stepped out of the bedroom, hugging the hallway wall, the .45's safety off, its hammer cocked.

Within a few minutes he had checked the bedrooms, the living room and kitchen and bathrooms, but there was no one here. They had left.

He pocketed the heavy automatic, then left by the front door and went back down to the parking lot.

"Find anything?" Roberta asked. She was nervous.

"He's gone," Carter said, climbing in behind the wheel. He looked up at the house.

"Back to Argentina?" she asked.

Carter looked at her and shook his head. "I'd guess Iceland. But you and I have to talk."

"About . . . ?"

"You and the BND. If we're going to work together, I'm going to have to know everything you have on Ziegler."

"And you're going to have to let me know what you have," she said. "A deal?"

Carter smiled. "A deal."

They shook hands. "Then what?" she asked as Carter started the car and they headed down the mountain.

"We're going to Iceland, that's what."

NINE

The drizzling rain was doing little to dispel the August heat as Nick and Roberta's plane touched down at National Airport in Washington late that evening. Perkins, one of Hawk's aides, was waiting for them outside customs. Carter had telephoned from the airport at Munich.

"You are expected, sir," Perkins said as he led them to the car. It was a code phrase meaning Hawk wanted to see Carter immediately.

"Get us over to my place first, Tom. Ms. Redgrave will be staying there."

"Yes, sir," the man said.

When they reached his building, Carter helped Roberta inside, and when she was settled in, he kissed her, promised he'd be back very soon, and went back to the car. He presumed she'd be calling the German embassy for instructions. He'd have Hawk straighten out that end of things.

As soon as Carter climbed in the car, Perkins headed away from the curb, a pinched look on his face.

"Trouble?" Carter asked.

"I think so, sir. They've been waiting for you. Mr. Hawk is very anxious."

"I see," Carter said. And a few minutes later they had made it across town to Dupont Circle where, as they turned the corner toward the entrance to the underground parking

133

ramp, he could see that the entire fifth floor of the Amalgamated Press building was lit up. Something big was going on.

Perkins dropped him in the underground lot, and Carter
signed in with the guard and took the elevator up to the fifth
floor. Hawk was waiting for him in the conference room
along with Jerry Baumgarten, head of the Western European
section of AXE, Bill Cairnes, technical division chief, and
John Starkey, liaison with the President's office. The four of
them looked grim.

"Are you all right?" Hawk asked, his voice gravelly. A
half-chewed cigar lay in the ashtray in front of him.

"I'm fit, sir," Carter said, taking a seat across the table.

"We've had a chance to look at the photographs," Hawk
said. "Now I want you to give us a complete update on
everything you've gotten into."

Carter had expected this, and he was ready. Quickly he
told them everything, beginning with the letter from Lydia
Coatsworth, his run-ins up in Iceland, and then the chain of
events in Argentina leading from Mendoza to Braga to Pepé,
and finally back to Mendoza who identified the man with the
monocle as Marc Ziegler.

"What about this Ziegler?" Baumgarten asked.

"He was an S.S. general. According to what I learned,
he's now a power within the Odessa."

Baumgarten looked pale. "Are you positive about this,
Nick?"

"Reasonably," Carter said, and he told them about the
Israeli in Buenos Aires who had provided the ID.

"That's it then," Baumgarten said to Hawk.

"What's 'it', sir?" Carter asked.

Cairnes sat forward. "The photographs you sent up here,
Carter, were most curious." The man was a brilliant scientist. "And disturbing."

"They're building a nuclear reactor in Iceland?" Carter
said. "With Odessa help?"

"That, as well as a waste material reprocessing plant.
Some of the equipment you photographed could be used for
nothing else."

"Reprocessing . . ." Carter started to say, but then he realized exactly what Cairnes was driving at, and his blood went cold. "Reprocessing of spent uranium fuel into weapons-grade material."

Cairnes nodded. "Those bastard ex-Nazis are building nuclear weapons."

"But why Iceland?"

Hawk broke in. "We're guessing now, Nick, but we think it's because a country such as Iceland would have had no trouble obtaining the international licenses to build a nuclear plant with outside help."

"Argentina certainly would not be granted such a permit," Baumgarten said.

"Evidently the Odessa has worked its way into Icelandic politics sufficiently to form such a partnership," Hawk said. "I don't think they realize who they're dealing with, but evidently the partnership is there."

"If the Nazis get the bomb . . ." Carter said, letting it trail off.

"Exactly," Hawk said. "I want you up there immediately. We're going to have to put a stop to it. ID section has a background worked up for you, as well as for Redgrave."

Carter perked up. "I was about to tell you about her, sir."

"No need," Hawk said. "Schmidt phoned this afternoon from Bonn. He's had Miss Redgrave working on this for some months now. She's on loan to our agency for the duration . . . that is if you want to work with her."

Carter grinned. "That'll be fine, sir, just fine."

Carter sat in a chair across from the bed, a drink in his hand. Roberta had been sleeping fitfully, and now she lay on her back, one hand flung above her head.

She had not telephoned her embassy; in fact, in the several hours Carter had been gone, she had done nothing but sleep.

She looked very young, Carter thought, watching her sleep. Too young and innocent to be involved in this business. Yet the dossier they had received from Schmidt, along with her bags that had been delivered to AXE, indicated she was very good. A pro.

She moaned again and rolled over. Sodium pentothol dreams, he thought. They recurred sometimes for months afterward. He'd been there, been chased by insane monsters with no possibility of escape.

After a while he turned on the light and came back to the bed. Beads of sweat glistened all along her hairline. "Roberta," he whispered.

Her eyes suddenly popped open and she sat bolt upright. "Nick," she exclaimed, throwing her arms around his neck. "Oh, God . . . I dreamed you had left me!"

"I just got back. Your things are here already."

"My things?" she asked, confused.

"From Schmidt. He sent them over. You'll be working with me officially now. We're leaving for Iceland in a few hours."

She pulled away. "I don't know . . ." she said vaguely, letting it trail off.

"You don't have to," Carter said. He had a fair idea what she was thinking.

"I told Ziegler everything I knew," she cried. She tried to hide her face in her hands, but Carter pulled them away.

"You're a professional," he said. "You know the hazards. It was sodium pentothol. There was nothing you could have done about it."

"I talked! I told him everything—like some babbling schoolgirl!"

"You were drugged!" Carter said. He got up, went back into the living room, and poured himself another cognac and one for Roberta.

"I really thought I had him," she said. She took the drink from Carter and sipped at it. "I really thought I'd wrap the case up soon." Her face was pale, and the muscles in her jaws were tight.

"There's something here you're not telling me, Roberta," Carter said. She *was* holding something back. He could see it in her eyes, and the way she held herself when she talked about Ziegler.

She said nothing.

"Is there some kind of personal thing?" he asked. "Have you got a vendetta against Ziegler?"

"No," she snapped.

"You're lying."

"Don't press me on this, Nick," she said. She got out of the bed, pushed past him, and went into the living room where she poured herself a second drink.

"We can't work together if you won't tell me the truth," Carter said. This was beginning to feel sour. If he were smart, he told himself, he'd have her pulled off the case and he'd do it alone.

"I just need a little time, Nick. But Ziegler has got to be stopped. He and men like him ruined my country, and very nearly the entire world. It can't be allowed to happen again."

He nodded. "All right," he said. "I'll give you the time, Roberta." He got up. "Get some more rest. I'm going to stretch out on the couch. We have to be out of here and to the airport by ten."

She nodded, and he went out to the living room. He turned off the light, tossed down the rest of his drink, and lay down on the couch.

For a long time he lay there, thinking about Roberta and about Ziegler and about going back to Iceland. Lydia had been murdered there. Of that there was no doubt now. If for nothing else, he told himself, he wanted to see this thing through to the end.

The bedroom door slowly opened, and Roberta came out. She was wearing nothing.

"Go back to bed," Carter said, half sitting up, but she came across to him and lay down beside him, her body cool and incredibly soft.

"Nick?" she sighed.

"Damn," Carter swore softly, but he didn't mean it. Soon he was undressed, and they were on the carpeted floor together, her long legs wrapped around his body, her lovely breasts crushed against his chest, and they were making love—slowly, tiredly, but with great comfort and pleasure.

They went into the bedroom together, where they finally got to sleep a couple of hours before dawn. When they woke, traffic was bustling in the street below, and it was already getting hot outside.

Carter got up and made coffee while Roberta showered and dressed. When she was ready he showered and dressed too. AXE had set him up with a new Luger, another stiletto in a chamois sheath, and a new gas bomb and pouch; in Germany, Schmidt had promised to see what he could do about finding Carter's original weapons. He packed these things in his suitcase so that he would have no trouble through Icelandic customs, and then he called a cab.

"Last night . . ." Roberta began on the way out to National Airport.

Carter smiled.

"It was lovely. I'm going to enjoy being your wife for this job. . . . I'm going to enjoy it a lot."

Carter had to laugh, the good feeling lasting all the way out to the airport, the hour-long wait there, and then the five-hour flight to Reykjavik.

When they touched down, however, the mood was gone. Completely. This was enemy territory, and they had a job to do.

The weather, particularly after the hot and sunny Washington morning, was terrible. Low, sullen-looking clouds hovered over the city, and a very chill wind blew in from the ocean.

They checked in at the Saga and registered under the names Angus and Marta McDonald. He was a salesman from Vancouver. He and his wife were here on a combined business trip and vacation.

They asked for and got a room on the top floor with a view of the harbor—which took several Canadian twenties—and when the bellboy left and Carter threw back the drapes covering the large windows, the entire harbor lay spread before them.

After room service had brought up a bottle of cognac and some sandwiches, Carter locked and chained the door, then set up a pair of high-powered binoculars on a tripod in front of the window. He pulled a chair over, sat down, and focused the glasses on the harbor. The ships leaped up at him. He could read the names with ease.

"I'll take the first shift," he said, pouring himself a drink and opening his notebook.

Roberta pecked him on the cheek. "I'll be a good little wifey and go shopping."

"Be careful," Carter said, and she left.

He locked the door after her, then went back to the binoculars. In his notebook he began drawing a detailed map of the harbor, along with the names and relative positions of every ship. When one came in, he added it; when one left, he scratched it.

There was a lot of activity in the harbor, so it kept him busy for several hours until Roberta came back and he let her in.

"Anything yet?" she asked. She had brought some more food and drink with her.

"Nothing suspicious," Carter said.

She put her packages down on the bureau and came over to where he was seated. She looked through the binoculars.

"If anything at all comes in from Argentina, from Ziegler's warehouses, we'll see it here," Carter said.

She looked away from the glasses. "That could take time."

Carter shrugged.

She made him a sandwich and opened a bottle of beer for him around four, when she took over the watch. He lay down on the bed for a while, watching the single Icelandic television channel.

A freighter, *The Delfin,* came in at six. But after she was tied up, nothing happened. No crew came to unload her.

Roberta watched until eight, then Carter took up the post again. The hotel window faced west into the harbor, into the setting sun; in Iceland, in August, the sun remains at the horizon for a very long time. The slanting rays played havoc with his vision.

At about eleven Carter fell asleep in the chair. Roberta was asleep in the bed, the television a static blank, having gone off at ten.

At 12:45 Carter woke with a start. Quickly he scanned the harbor, then trained his glasses on *The Delfin*. Something was happening. He sat up straighter. Lights were on over the ship's hold, and a gigantic crane was swinging a load onto the dock, where a heavy truck was waiting to receive it.

"Roberta," Carter called.

She sat up, rubbed her eyes, then came over to the glasses. "What is it?" she asked sleepily.

"Take a look," he said, getting up.

She looked through the binoculars. "*The Delfin*," she said. "They're unloading something. . . . Is it what I think it is?"

"Possibly," Carter said. He had pulled his weapons out of his specially designed radio-cassette player. He strapped them on now.

Roberta grabbed her bag, and together they hurried downstairs to the hotel parking lot, where they retrieved the car they'd rented and headed immediately toward the dock where *The Delfin* was tied.

"If they're unloading reactor parts, they'll be taking them out to the construction site."

"Maybe they haven't started yet," Roberta said. "Maybe they're just stockpiling the equipment until they're ready."

Carter shook his head. "Hawk and I have already discussed that possibility. From what we can learn, discussions in the Althing about the nuclear alternative have stalled. The Odessa cannot take the chance it'll be defeated, not at this stage of the game, so it's my guess they've already started construction. When Iceland's geothermal energy does run out, they'll unveil the reactor. A fait accompli, and the Althing will have no choice but to accept it.''

"A dangerous game."

"Exactly. It's why Ziegler and his people will stop at nothing to protect it.''

The streets near the docks were dark and empty. Carter pulled up and parked in the shadows beside a warehouse.

The Delfin is just around the corner, I think,'' Carter said. The other side was lit up. "I'm going to take a look. Give me fifteen minutes, then get the hell out of here.''

She pulled a small Beretta automatic out of her purse, then nodded. "Careful.''

Carter went the rest of the way on foot, and at the corner he looked out across the dock. The truck had been loaded. As he watched, the driver and another man climbed up into the cab, started the big diesel, and the truck lumbered forward.

Carter had to duck back out of the way as the truck passed, but then he raced back to the car where Roberta was behind the wheel.

He jumped in on the passenger side. "That's it,'' he shouted. "Don't lose him.''

Roberta started the car and screeched away from their parking place, picking up the truck's headlights in the next block.

TEN

The truck led them south of Reykjavik, down a little-used two-lane blacktop. There was absolutely no other traffic, and only the glow of the city behind them lent any evidence to the fact that civilization was near.

"Cut your lights and stay with him," Carter said.

The big transport disppeared over the crest of a hill. Carter and Roberta reached the top minutes later, but the valley beyond was empty. The truck was nowhere to be seen.

"Where'd it go?" Roberta asked, slowing down.

"There," Carter said, picking out a rooster tail of dust on a track that trailed off the highway between twin mounds of pumice.

Roberta turned off the pavement, and they slowly bumped along the uneven track. This was volcano country. Carter unfolded the map that had come with the car and studied it for several moments with the aid of his penlight. Ahead was an oddly shaped, flat-topped cone.

"Mount Hekla," he said.

"Isn't that the one that erupted not so long ago?" Roberta asked.

"In 1973," Carter read from the inscription on the map.

The truck suddenly appeared as they came around a bend in the road. Its brake lights were on, and Carter cautioned her to slow down and then stop. In the dim Arctic twilight he could barely make out the shape of a guardhouse on the road ahead.

"It's a checkpoint," he said. He turned around and looked the way they had come. "We'd better turn around here and see if there is some way around it."

She made a quick U-turn and backtracked nearly half a mile until they came to what appeared to be a very old track in the sand leading off to the east. She swung on to it and carefully picked her way around huge boulders strewn everywhere.

"This is nothing but a dried creek bed," she shouted. The car was bouncing and pitching all over the place. The car wouldn't take much of this.

"Can we make it to the top of the ridge ahead?" Carter shouted.

"I'll try."

They bottomed out several times, and the temperature gauge began to climb as the car labored over the extremely rough terrain.

The ridge, when they reached it, turned out to be the rim of a wide, shallow canyon. Lights twinkled far out in its center.

They eased up over the final rise and stopped. Roberta shut off the engine. "What is it?" she asked, looking down at the floor of the canyon.

"I'm not sure," Carter said. He got out of the car and walked to the edge of the overlook. A hundred yards down the hill a chain link fence ran along the landscape, topped by three strands of barbed wire. On the other side a huge hole had been dug out of the valley, and in the distance he could see that some sort of huge building project was rising. The wind brought sounds of engines running.

He motioned for Roberta, and when she joined him she strained to listen. "They're working on it now." She looked at Carter. "You were right after all; they've already started it."

"And we're going to un-start it," Carter said.

"How?"

"I don't know, but . . ." Carter started to say when a movement below, just at the fence, caught his eye. "Down," he whispered urgently, and he shoved Roberta down behind a jumble of rocks.

"What is it?" she whispered.

"A guard, I think," Carter said. As he watched a uniformed guard sauntered along the fence from the west. An automatic rifle was slung over his shoulder. It looked like an M-16.

He stopped for a moment or two almost directly below them, then continued on. When he was out of sight, Carter sat back.

"It's a reactor, all right, and probably the processing plant for the spent fuel rods as well," he said.

"Odessa's own little bomb factory," Roberta said. "So how do we stop it?"

"We blow it up, what else?"

They got back to the hotel a couple of hours later, after they had hiked along the fence line for a short distance so that they could get a better view of what was going on below.

Carter dropped Roberta off, telling her to keep watch on the harbor, but he refused to tell her where he was going despite her indignant questions.

"Are you going back out there tonight?" she demanded.

"No, I promise you, Roberta. I'll be back in a couple of hours."

She looked at him. "What do you plan to do alone? I want a chance at Ziegler for what he did to me," she said.

"You'll have it. I'm not doing anything tonight except gathering information. Nothing more."

After he left her, Carter drove immediately across town to the American embassy on Laufasvegi, where he woke up a sleepy chancellery clerk who telephoned the chargé d'affaires; the chargé d'affaires checked with the ambassador himself, and the ambassador ended up calling in the embassy's chief military officer.

"Do you realize what time of the morning it is?" the officer, an air force colonel, fumed when he arrived.

"Thank you for coming down on such short notice, Colonel," Carter said.

"What do you want?"

"The use of your crypto facilities."

"What?"

"I need to set up a crypto teletype circuit with D.C. It can be routed through the Pentagon."

"Impossible," the officer said.

They were sitting in the chancellery office. Carter turned to the clerk. "Telephone the ambassador for me like a good sport."

"Yes, sir," the man said, and he reached for the telephone.

"I suppose you have the clout," the colonel said. The clerk hesitated.

"Yes," Carter said. "But if you want to check with someone, I'll understand."

"It's not necessary; the ambassador vouched for you. Highly irregular, though, I might say."

They went down to the basement, where the colonel and Carter were let into a small room filled with electronic equipment. The colonel explained Carter's needs to the young technician on duty, and Carter supplied the routing code for the circuit he wanted.

Within fifteen minutes it was set up, and Carter had an encrypted teletype line open with AXE's technical section in the basement of the Dupont Circle building.

The colonel and the tech moved off to the other side of the room while Carter operated the teletype.

CARTER HERE FOR CAIRNES

STAND BY N3

Carter sat back and lit a cigarette. It was one of his

custom-made cigarettes that he picked up from a small shop around the corner from his apartment building. The paper was black, and his initials were stamped in gold near the tip.

Cairnes was back before Carter finished his smoke.

CAIRNES HERE
HAVE YOU SOMETHING FOR ME?

As completely as possible, Carter described for the head of AXE's technical section what he and Roberta had seen outside Reykjavik.

When he was finished, the teletype was silent for nearly an hour until Cairnes came back on.

UNITS YOU DESCRIBE ARE PROBABLE
REACTOR TO WEST
PROCESSING PLANT NEAREST
PERIMETER.
WHAT DO YOU DESIRE, N3?

Carter smiled to himself He typed:

MEANS FOR CERTAIN DESTRUCTION.

STAND BY.

Again the teletype was silent for at least an hour. The colonel had become fidgety, and he finally left. The tech remained across the room, his feet up, reading a magazine, totally unconcerned about Carter.

When the teletype came to life again, it clattered at a hundred words per minute. The chief scientist had evidently cut a tape and was running it off now.

COMMENTS ON METHODS OF
DESTROYING A NUCLEAR REACTOR
AND/OR A NUCLEAR FUEL PROCESSING
INSTALLATION.

IF THE CORE IS ALREADY IN PLACE
DESTRUCTION OF THE REACTOR COULD
LEAD TO SERIOUS AIR AND WATER
CONTAMINATION LOCALLY.

IN AN EFFORT TO INSURE COMPLETE
DESTRUCTION AND NOT MERELY A
DELAY IN CONSTRUCTION,
CONSIDERATION MUST BE GIVEN TO THE
VULNERABLE AREAS.

AT THE BASE OF THE REACTOR CORE
ITSELF WILL BE SEEN A LARGE BLOCK OF
REINFORCED CONCRETE WHICH
SUPPORTS THE MECHANISM WHICH IN
TURN CONTROLS THE CONTROL RODS.

DESTRUCTION OF THIS CONSTRUCTION
COULD RESULT IN A MAXIMUM DELAY IN
CONSTRUCTION FOR THE MINIMUM USE
OF FORCE.

SPECIFICATIONS TO FOLLOW.

Carter lit another cigarette as the teletype spewed out various specifications for explosives, for placing the charges, and for probable effects.

When it was finished, Carter teletyped back his acknowledgment, then shut down the circuit. He reread the instructions, then pulled off the paper, the carbon, and the ribbon, and brought them to the shredder set up in one corner where he destroyed them.

"Get the colonel back down here, if you would," he asked the tech, and by the time he had finished destroying the message and copy, the colonel was back.

Carter quickly explained what he needed, and within

half an hour, his trunk loaded with plastique and the timers, he drove back to the hotel and parked at the back of the lot.

He went up to their room. Roberta had been asleep, but she woke up when he came in.

"You're back," she sighed sleepily, and she came into his arms.

He kissed her neck, and she moaned deep in her throat as she moved even closer. "Nick?" she said.

He pushed her back, then kissed the nipples of her breasts, her flat stomach, and soon they were making love, her body soft and yielding, while at the same moment one part of his mind was thinking about the night to come.

It was going to be difficult to get close enough to plant the plastique. Besides the fence, which he was reasonably certain was alarmed, there wasn't a hell of a lot of cover out there. A few rocks here and there, but no tall grass or trees or anything of that sort.

He didn't think there was any way around their personnel security. He did not think he'd be able to get in through the front gate. Not this time. No . . . it would have to be over or through the fence. Down the hill. Plant the charges. And then get the hell out.

By that night, when for the second time in twenty-four hours they had driven up the dry creek bed toward the rim overlooking the installation, Carter was ready to move. He had a debt to pay for the way Ziegler had treated them, and he meant to return it tonight.

He parked the car well down from the lip of the rim after he had turned it around. He was not planning on coming out the same way he got in. Once he breached the fence, the alarms would sound, and the clock would begin ticking. He'd not have a lot of time to get down to the reactor site, plant the charges, and then get clear.

The one plus point, however, was that while he was making a retreat in the opposite direction, the perimeter security people would be concentrating on his entry point.

He shut off the car and turned to Roberta. "I want you to return to the hotel. If I'm not back by morning, I want you to get in contact with your boss. Tell him what happened. He'll contact mine."

She had argued earlier that she had wanted to go with him. But he had told her no. She tried again.

"I told you I wanted to be a part of it," she said.

"And I told you that when I went after Ziegler you'd be able to help. Right now I'm just going to put a damper on his reactor, that's all. He'll come later."

"Watch yourself, Nick. I want there to be a later."

Carter smiled, kissed her, then got out of the car. He opened the trunk and pulled out the pack containing the plastique and detonators, as well as the large wire cutters.

He shouldered the pack, then slammed the trunk, and scrambled up the hill where Roberta was crouched behind a rock.

"He just went by," she whispered.

"Wish me luck," he said, and kissed her again.

"Luck," Roberta said as he scrambled away from the rock and down the hundred yards to the fence.

He could hear the sounds of construction machinery below in the valley, but nothing else. Crouching next to the fence, he raised the wire cutters, hesitated for just a moment, then cut the first strand.

There were no alarms, no sparks or lights, nothing. But as he cut strand after strand of the wire mesh fence, he was certain that somewhere within the huge compound a light was flashing, pinpointing exactly where the fence had been penetrated.

When he had the hole large enough, he tossed the wire cutters back up the hill, waved to Roberta, then ducked through the hole and took off in a crouching run down the hill.

"Good luck," he heard her call from behind, and then he

was out of earshot as he hurried toward the first line of
buildings that made up the perimeter of the vast complex.

Roberta watched until he was out of sight, then walked
back over the crest of the hill to where the car was parked.
She stripped off her jumpsuit. Underneath she wore a summer dress with a V-neck that accentuated the deep milky
white of her cleavage. She smoothed the wrinkles from the
dress with her hands, and from beneath the seat she pulled out a
pair of high-heeled shoes. She untied the sneakers she was
wearing and slipped on the dressy sandals. Her makeup was
in her handbag, which she dug out and applied in the rearview
mirror. When she felt she was ready, she started the car and
drove back to the main road, but instead of turning left into
town, she went right, toward the checkpoint into the complex.

Halfway there she stopped the car, shut off the engine,
got out, and raised the hood. She reached in and gently pulled
two wires from their sockets in the distributor cap. Then she
closed the hood and got back behind the wheel. When she got
the car started again, the engine was sputtering and bucking.

By the time she reached the gate, the car was backfiring
every tenth or twelfth revolution, and clouds of unburned
gasoline were being expelled from the exhaust. She let it
bang a final time, cut the engine, and let it coast to within
twenty-five yards of the guardhouse.

She tried the starter twice to no avail. She was about to try
it a third time when she heard a soft tapping at the window.

She looked up. A guard was there, an automatic slung over
his shoulder. She rolled down the window. "Where is this?"
she asked in English.

"Is something wrong with your car, miss?" the guard
asked, his German accent strong in his halting English.

"It keeps stalling. I turned off the main road. I saw the
lights. I need help."

"This is a government installation," the man said, his

eyes straying to her breasts.

"Perhaps you could help me," she said. "I know nothing about cars."

He smiled and licked his lips.

"I would be ever so grateful," she purred.

He went around to the front of the car. She pulled the hood release, then got out. A second guard had come from the gate. She could see no others in the small guardhouse.

"Can you see what the problem is?" she asked, coming around to the front. She pulled her Beretta nine-shot automatic from her purse.

"There are wires loose . . ." the guard started to say.

Roberta turned around and shot the guard by the gate two times. When he started to go down she turned back. As the guard under the hood was scrambling for the rifle over his shoulder, she shot him once through the side of the head.

He fell forward onto the engine, then turned and slumped to the pavement, hanging at an absurd angle from his rifle strap which had become tangled in the bumper.

Working quickly, Roberta unhooked him, then dragged him by the cuffs onto the road shoulder and into the rocky field beyond. She hurried back to the gate and dragged the second guard out into the field. She took their weapons, returned to the car, reattached the spark plug wires, then drove several hundred feet off the road into the darkness.

The guards had left the gate ajar. She slipped through the opening with a delicious, coppery taste of fear at the back of her throat. But her purse swung as she walked through, hitting the steel mesh of the gate. Inside the guardhouse a light began to flash.

ELEVEN

A siren began wailing into the night air when Carter was less than a hundred feet from the massive reactor control rod support column, and he had to duck behind a pile of concrete forms.

Men, momentarily confused, scrambled through the work area in response to the alarm. But Carter had no doubts that they would begin a systematic search for the intruder at any minute. He didn't have a hell of a lot of time now to do what he had come for.

One of the construction workers raced by him, and Carter reached out, tripping the man. Before the other had a chance to react, Carter was on him, knocking him unconscious.

Quickly he dressed in the man's dark coveralls and hard hat, then jumped up and started toward the control rod base at the same moment that a half-dozen workmen and a couple of armed guards headed his way.

He had to turn away, and he hurried off at an angle, ducking around to the front of a small wooden shed that looked like a privy. It was set apart from the other buildings, and the sign on the front door told him why: GEFAHR EXPLOSIV was painted in large red letters.

At the moment, no one was paying him any attention, so he slipped inside the tiny shed. It was warm inside, and the still air reeked of cordite. Against one wall, cases of dynamite reached nearly to the low ceiling.

Carter pulled one of the cases off the pile and pried open its lid with his stiletto. Below a layer of sawdust lay a row of twenty dynamite sticks. There were other rows beneath that one.

He looked up at the other cases. There certainly was enough firepower here to level a good portion of the construction.

Quickly he searched the other boxes and the few items on the shelves. There was, in addition to the dynamite, plenty of electrical wire, several plungers, tape, and several drills for opening blast holes in the rock. There were no blasting caps, however. For safety's sake the caps were evidently stored in another location. It made sense, but it also made things difficult.

With great care Carter pulled off his pack and stuffed a dozen sticks of dynamite in with the lump of plastique in the square package.

The alarm sirens suddenly stopped, and he went to the door and looked outside. A squad of gray-coveralled guards doubled-timed up the road past him and deeper into the construction area. They immediately fanned out and slowed down, shining flashlights into every nook and cranny. They knew someone was in the area. And they were going to find him.

Carter slipped out of the storage shed and struck out in the opposite direction, keeping low behind the mechanized equipment and the other storage sheds. He headed toward a single-story, horseshoe-shaped building he'd seen on the way in. A patch of grass had been planted in front, and the flag of Iceland flew from a staff.

Housing, he thought. He looked back over his shoulder toward the core support. Before he could get close enough to his objective to do any damage, he'd have to create a diversion.

He hurried the rest of the way across the field to the building, where he looked in one of the windows. It was a barracks. Metal cots lined the walls, each neatly made, a trunk at the foot. It looked very much like a typical military installation. No one was in sight. Everyone had evidently been mustered out to search for him.

He moved around the end of the building, along the back wall, until he came to a loading dock with cases of food stacked up. A set of double screen doors gave entrance to a large kitchen.

He looked inside. Racks of pots and pans hung over gleaming metal counters reflected in a bank of brushed steel refrigerators that ran along the wall. The kitchen too was deserted. Apparently even the cooks were expected to muster out in an emergency. But they hadn't expected to be gone very long. At the far end of the room a stew pot bubbled on a burner of one of the ranges.

Carter hurried across the kitchen to the stove and studied the controls for a moment or two. He smiled. If a diversion was needed, a diversion was what they would get.

He pulled off his pack, took out the dynamite, and placed the sticks in the oven. He closed the door, then turned the oven control to five hundred degrees.

It wouldn't take very long. Perhaps half a minute. Sixty seconds tops.

He hurried out of the kitchen and dashed across the access road toward a cluster of buildings on the other side of a shallow drainage ditch. The front gate lay only a few hundred yards beyond.

A lone guard ambled aimlessly up the dirt road from the construction area, his machine gun in his hands. He spotted Carter coming across the field.

"Halt! *Halten sie!*" he shouted, pulling his gun around and firing.

Slugs kicked up dust to the left of Carter as he sprinted right, racing toward one of the mobile offices perched on cinder blocks.

He plunged under it as the guard shouted something else, then scrambled on his belly to the other side. Immediately he leaped atop the propane tanks supplying the trailer. The guard would be looking for him . . . or at least for his feet.

The guard pulled up short on the other side. For a moment there was silence. *"Wo ist?"* the man shouted.

A police whistle sounded in the construction area. They had heard the shooting. But where the hell was the dynamite? Hadn't the oven come on?

Carter peered around the edge of the trailer. At least twenty men were racing up the access road by the barracks. He turned back. Behind him the nearest cover was a building a hundred yards away . . . across an open field that afforded absolutely no cover. Beyond that was what appeared to be a motor pool, cars, jeeps and trucks parked everywhere.

The guard was coming around the trailer when a great roar tore the air, shoving the trailer half off its blocks. As Carter fell to the ground he had visions of the trailer falling over on him. He scrambled away from it as he pulled out his Luger.

The sky was raining debris; starry bits of flaming wood, and bits of metal and rock and sand poured down as the entire far side of the barracks building burned furiously, flames shooting high into the sky.

The guard who had followed him came the rest of the way around the trailer in a dead run. When he saw Carter he lifted his machine gun. In one smooth motion Carter raised his Luger and squeezed off a shot, catching the man in the chest. He went down.

The guards who had been coming up the road were lying scattered on the gravel. They had been just behind the kitchen when the dynamite went off.

Carter turned and sprinted across the field in the direction of the motor pool.

Ziegler's new secretary, a blonde who had been hired here in Iceland, stood at the window watching the fire when Roberta came into the outer office.

"Oh," the girl said, spinning around. Her face seemed blank.

"I'm the masseuse," Roberta said.

The girl just shook her head.

"I was called."

"Oh, yes, of course," the girl said, and she sat down behind her desk and shifted through some papers.

Roberta knew what she would find. Ziegler had a standing appointment for "massage therapy" every evening at this time . . . or at least he had in Buenos Aires. She had followed her hunch earlier in the day and had hit pay dirt.

In Argentina she had even made the calls for Ziegler—to the local pimps—but here in Iceland she had had to make a dozen calls before she finally found the massage service that Ziegler was using. She told the service that she was Ziegler's secretary and requested that they cancel that evening's appointment.

"The agency called . . . said it was canceled for some reason," the girl said. "He called me to come in to see if I couldn't find someone . . . but then, the fire."

The girl seemed bewildered.

"I'm the replacement," Roberta said, winging it. She hadn't thought the massage service would have telephoned. But this girl wasn't too bright.

"You are?" the girl said hopefully.

"Yes," Roberta said. She looked around. "Which way to . . ."

The girl jumped up. "Just a minute, please. I'll tell him you've come after all." She disappeared through a door, and Roberta went to the window and looked outside. Whatever Nick had blown up was burning furiously. It would keep Ziegler's guards occupied for some time. Sooner or later, of course, it would be discovered that the two on the main gate were gone. When that happened, all hell would break loose.

"He's just about ready for you," the secretary said. "If you'll just come with me . . ."

Roberta followed the woman through the door and down a short, plushly carpeted corridor to a small dressing room, mirrors on all the walls.

"You can change in here," the secretary said, leaving

Roberta and closing the door behind her.

Ziegler liked his sexual encounters kinky. The weirder the better. For months she had been his procurer, so she knew his likes and dislikes fairly well, as disgusting as they were. But they were his one major weakness.

She quickly peeled off her clothes and stepped into the costume she had bought at a small shop in a seedier section of Reykjavik: metal-studded, black leather bra and panties with cutouts in strategic places, black fishnet nylons, and tall, imitation leather stiletto-heeled boots.

From her large purse she pulled out a red wig and put it on, redid her makeup, then stepped back and looked critically at herself in the mirror. She had worked with Ziegler for some time, but she didn't think he had ever really looked at her. It had been his goons, not him, who had interrogated her. He was almost always too busy, in too much of a hurry. And now, the change in her appearance was startling. Besides, she shuddered, the holes in the costume exposed the nipples of her breasts and her pubis. She didn't think he'd even notice her face.

From her purse she extracted a razor-sharp knife, which she shoved down her left boot, then sighed deeply and opened the door.

"Herr Ziegler," she called out, but there was no answer. She stepped out into the corridor. To the left was the door that led back to the outer office. To the right was another door. She turned right.

At the door she put her ear to the wood and listened. There was nothing at first, and she was about to open the door when a telephone rang from within.

It was answered a moment later by Ziegler; she recognized his voice.

"Have you got him yet?" he demanded.

Roberta felt very exposed standing here. At any moment someone could come from the outer office.

"I want the entire core area totally surrounded. Bring up the big lights from engineering. Whatever happens, he cannot be allowed anywhere near the core, the building, the plumbing, or especially the core support. Your life depends upon that. Do I make myself clear?''

Damn, Roberta thought. Nick didn't have a chance of getting close now. She only hoped that he'd manage to get clear.

"Don't call me back until you have him," Ziegler said, and she could hear him slam down the phone.

She took a deep breath, let it out slowly, then knocked a couple of times and walked in.

Ziegler had been standing by the window. He spun around, his jaw dropping when she flounced in.

"There you are," she squealed, shutting the door when she was inside. "I waited and waited, but you never came."

Ziegler seemed flustered. It was very much out of his ordinary character, but then he liked to play these games.

"I'm . . . sorry, my dear," he whimpered almost contritely. "There was the phone call . . . and . . ." He let his voice trail off.

Roberta came around the desk and stood in front of him, her legs spread, her hands on her hips. She could see how excited he was becoming. Her heart was hammering. She had waited for a moment such as this for a very long time. Ever since she had learned that Ziegler was one of the men from Dachau. One of the killers there, where her mother had just barely survived with her life.

Ziegler had been her mother's lover. She had been kept in the camp brothel for the exclusive use of General Martel Zimmerman. He had brought her presents and good things to eat at first, but later his sexual appetites began to take on a new twist.

Painfully her mother had explained it all to her teenage daughter shortly before her death in the early sixties. It was a story she had never been able to tell her husband.

Looking now at Ziegler made her stomach turn. But her mother's story came back to her although she wanted to bury it.

At first he had used chains and whips on her mother. And then cigarette burns and finally even a soldering iron between her toes, in her armpits, in her anus, and on the lips of her vagina. The pain was so terrible, her mother remembered with tears in her eyes, but it was nothing compared to what came later.

He began to change, her mother said, slowly and subtly at first. He used to tie her up, but one time he forgot, and she struck out blindly, hitting him in the face.

He reared back, and she was certain that she would die that instant, but he was smiling. He had enjoyed it.

A few weeks later the same thing happened again, and this time she scratched him. He seemed to be in ecstasy.

During the months that followed, the transformation came faster and faster until at last she was handcuffing him, whipping him, and even urinating on him. At one point she was even cutting him with a knife.

The terrible thing about it, her mother remembered, was that by then she had been his prisoner for more than two years. She could have easily killed him during one of those sessions, but she had been changed so much by him that she merely did as he asked. She tortured him, abused him, kicked and screamed at him; it was the only way he could get sexual satisfaction.

Nothing had changed.

"Get down on your hands and knees, you swine," Roberta hissed. She meant it, and Ziegler loved it.

He got to his knees and bowed his head. "You must forgive me, my dear. The telephone . . ."

Roberta kicked him in the chest, sending him staggering backward, off-balance.

He grinned. "You're a feisty whore. . . . I like that! More!"

Roberta reared back and kicked him in the chest again, just beneath his left breast. The air went out of him, and he fell back on the floor behind the desk.

She advanced on him as he began to laugh, long and low,

the sound totally devoid of humor. He was some kind of a monster.

"What do you want now, Herr Ziegler?" she snapped.

He laughed louder. "Delicious," he said. "Oh . . . God, it's so delicious. You're so much like your mother, my dear. So much . . . you'll never know."

Roberta's heart froze. Her knees suddenly felt weak, and she felt very obscene standing over Ziegler in the costume she was wearing.

He knew! Oh, God, he had known all along! He had waited for just this moment.

She reached down and quickly pulled the knife from her boot, but Ziegler had sat up, and he grabbed her right ankle with a meaty paw and jerked it out from under her.

She fell back, banging her shoulder on the edge of the desk, losing her grip on the knife. It went clattering across the floor, and Ziegler was on her.

"You want to hurt me, my dear?" he asked, breathing heavily. "That can be arranged. But later. I think first we'll have to soften you up a bit. Maybe take a month or two. Who knows, maybe it'll take eighteen months like with your mother the whore."

She struggled out of his grasp and scrambled backward across the floor to where the knife lay. But the office door burst open at that moment, and four guards, all of them armed, their weapons at the ready, came in.

One of them yanked Roberta to her feet, while the others helped Ziegler up.

He came to where she stood, and without warning reached out with the little knife and cut her bra so it fell from her body.

She struggled wildly. "Hold her," Ziegler barked. A second guard came over, and together with the other one they held Roberta still. Her stomach was churning. Oh, Nick, she thought. She had been such a fool.

Ziegler pulled off her panties, her boots, and the mesh nylons, leaving her nude.

"Nice?" he asked his guards. They were all leering at her.

"Your orders are simple, gentlemen," Ziegler said. "Take this whore over to Barracks B and teach her just what fine, strong men you are." He smiled at Roberta. "I certainly don't want her killed, nor do I want her damaged . . . too badly. Just have a little fun, that's all."

TWELVE

The flames from the burning barracks were already beginning to die down when Carter made it to the motor pool area. He crouched just behind the large maintenance garage as he listened and watched for the sign of a guard or guards.

He didn't think anyone would be here. Everyone would be back by the barracks or by the reactor site. Yet he didn't want to be caught again as he had been back at the trailer.

Ziegler had been a lot smarter than Carter had given him credit for being. The explosion at the barracks, instead of being a diversion, had caused Ziegler's men to concentrate on the vulnerable reactor. A barracks could be replaced. If the reactor core was destroyed, the project would be all but finished.

After he had gotten away from the trailer, Carter had seen dozens, perhaps even a hundred or more men all heading toward the reactor site. It would be difficult now, if not impossible to get close. But he had to try.

He holstered his Luger and pulled out his stiletto, then, keeping low, raced away from the building toward a line of a half-dozen jeeps and several heavy-duty trucks parked near the gas pumps.

He jumped up on the running board of one of the trucks, got in behind the wheel, and ducked under the dashboard. He pulled out his penlight and shined it up on the wires around the ignition switch. In less than a minute he had hot-wired the truck, and it started up with a roar.

He sat up, pulling the pack around, and opened it up on the seat next to him. He pulled out the plastique, and working quickly but very carefully, he inserted the timer into the lump of claylike explosive. He set this one beside him, then took the second plastique brick and detonator out, and inserted the detonator into the explosive.

He jumped out of the truck, went around to the gas pumps, and molded the brick against the base of the center one. He set the timer for sixty seconds, raced back to the truck, put it in gear, and ground away from the motor pool.

As he came around the corner of the big maintenance building, he slammed the truck into second gear and accelerated up the rough construction road toward the reactor area half a mile away.

There were a lot of lights shining around the scaffolding and tall cement forms. The core building itself, along with the supports, was completely bathed in spotlights. As he drove he could pick out dozens of troops ringing the building.

He flipped on his lights, pulled his hard hat low, and jammed the accelerator pedal to the floor, the big truck bucking and swaying over the deeply rutted dirt track. The gas pumps blew with a tremendous flash.

There were a half-dozen medics around the fallen troops behind the barracks, which was still burning, and they looked up for just a moment as Carter passed but immediately went back to what they were doing.

Carter cranked down the window on his side as he swung back up toward the reactor building, and with one hand set the timer for ninety seconds.

He was going to have one pass at this, and that was it. He didn't think much of his chances for success, but he just couldn't let it go.

The detonator was ticking as he closed in on the reactor building. Four guards came out from behind some scaffolding, and they began to wave for Carter to stop. He swung a little further left so that he would come even closer to the core support.

The guards raised their weapons at the last moment and started firing, the windshield shattering as Carter ducked down.

Then he was past them. He straightened up and tossed the plastique out the window with all his might, but it fell short.

He just caught a glimpse of the package lying on the ground as he came around the main reactor building, made a wide turn on two wheels, and headed directly for the main gate.

He was counting out loud to ninety. He was off. At eighty-four the night sky behind him was split with a tremendous explosion.

The damage he had done here tonight would keep them busy for a little while. But he failed to destroy the core. There'd have to be another time . . . one way or the other.

Carter got the impression that there were no guards on duty, and that the main gate had been unlocked, when without stopping or even slowing down he crashed out to the dirt road that led down to the highway. But then he was past and careening away from the huge compound, already making plans for his second attempt. He and Roberta would have to get away from the hotel they were staying at, of course. Ziegler would have his people crawling all over town by morning. The man would stop at nothing, Carter was sure.

He made it down to the highway a few minutes later and checked his rearview mirror to make sure no one was following him. Then he turned left toward Reykjavik and accelerated smoothly through the gears.

He took off the hard hat and tossed it aside, then lit a cigarette. For just a moment he had the ugly thought that Roberta might have tried something tonight on her own. She had acted strangely on the way out, and earlier in the day, when he had been watching the harbor, he had looked up once to find that she had left the room. She had been out shopping . . . but for what?

But he dismissed the thought. She wanted Ziegler—although she wouldn't explain to him exactly why—but he didn't think she wanted him so badly she'd jeopardize this mission. She was more of a professional than that.

He settled back for the long ride into the city, his mind slowly going over everything that had happened so far on this strange operation. He thought back as well to Lydia Coatsworth. Even now, after all that had gone on, he found it nearly impossible to believe she was dead. And he had to admit to himself that he had really felt very deeply about her. Perhaps too deeply for a man in his occupation.

There was virtually no traffic on the highway until he came within a few miles of Reykjavik itself, and then there was only an occasional car or truck, and one bus.

He parked the big truck outside a heavy equipment service center, pulled off the coveralls, and then walked a mile and a half up to the Sudurlandsbraut, near the sports grounds, where he hitched a ride with a truck driver returning to the Telephone and Telegraphic office.

The man said something to Carter in Icelandic, but when he realized that Carter was an American he drove the rest of the way in dark silence. Like many Icelanders, he did not care for Americans. Although there were treaties between the two countries, outlining fishing rights, as well as allowing American military bases here, Icelanders mistrusted America's interests. Too many other countries had been swallowed, economically, by the giant to the south, and in the process had lost their national identities. Icelanders did not want that happening here.

He dropped Carter off downtown, then hurried way down the street and around the corner, Carter walked the two blocks to his hotel, went in the back way, took the stairs up, and knocked on his door.

''Roberta?'' he called out softly. There was no answer, so he knocked a little louder. She had to be back by now, he thought, unless. . . .

He pulled out his stiletto and picked the lock. The room

was dark. He flipped on the light, half expecting to see evidence of a search, but nothing had been disturbed.

Locking the door behind him, he crossed the room and looked into the bathroom. Roberta had not been back. Damnit, she was still out there.

He turned and was about to leave when the corner of an envelope sticking out from beneath his pillow caught his eye. Even before he opened it he knew what it was: Roberta's explanation of why she wasn't there.

It was that, but it was much more than he expected. She had written him a lengthy letter that began by asking him to forgive her and please understand why she was doing what she was doing.

He poured himself a stiff drink as he read Roberta's account of what had happened to her mother during the war.

"So you see, Nick darling, I must kill him in the same way he caused the death of my mother's spirit," she concluded.

She was still out there.

He finished his drink, stuffed the letter into his pocket, and threw open the door but stopped short, the barrel of a .357 magnum poking him in the chest, a giant of a man with blue eyes and blond hair standing there. Behind him was another giant of a man and Thorstein Josepsson.

"I was wondering when I'd run into you again," Carter said.

"I told you to stay away, Mr. Angus McDonald, or Nick Carter, or whoever you really are. I told you not to become involved in our politics."

"So now you're going to kill me?"

"Not I," Josepsson said. "Not unless you force us to do it. But there is someone who would very much like to speak with you."

The second giant stepped forward and quickly frisked Carter, finding his Luger but neither Hugo nor Pierre. He pocketed the weapon after first removing its clip and the shell from the chamber.

"I would rather you come peacefully with us," Josepsson

said. "If you would choose otherwise, of course, we could break a limb or two, and take you out on a stretcher."

"I can't argue with firepower," Carter said. "Besides, I'm curious about who would like to see me."

They walked down the corridor together, Josepsson in the lead, used the rear stairs, and went outside to a large Mercedes limousine. A driver was waiting for them. Josepsson got in the front seat, and Carter was sandwiched in the back between his two guards. From the expression on their faces, he was sure they'd just as soon kill him here and now as look at him.

Rounding the hotel, they headed southwest to a section of large, lovely homes set back in the hills. Each home had a view of the city and of the ocean beyond. It was spectacular.

The sun was just beginning to come up when the driver pulled through an electrically-controlled gate and drove slowly up a long, curving driveway. He parked behind a very large three-story red-brick home, almost large enough to be considered a mansion.

Josepsson got out first. "Bring him into the study. I'll see if the general has returned yet," he said, and he disappeared into the house.

One of the guards got out of the car, then reached in, grabbed Carter by the collar, and yanked him out of the back seat. The other giant got out behind him. They went up the porch, into the house, and down a short corridor into a much larger, much wider hallway, where they directed him through a set of double doors into a large, book-lined study.

They shoved him into an easy chair, then they both stepped back toward the door, folded their arms over their chests, and watched him.

"Lovely weather we've been having, isn't it?" Carter said, looking around the room. Behind him, curtains covered what he assumed to be large windows or possibly even French doors. Aside from the door they had come through, another much narrower door led off to the side. A private exit to the rest of the house, perhaps? "What?" Carter looked back at the guards. "Cat got your tongues? Pity."

"Large does not mean stupid, Mr. Carter of the U.S. intelligence service," one of them said. His accented English was definitely Oxford.

"Mind if I stretch my legs?" Carter asked, starting to get up.

'The moment you lose contact with that chair, you are a dead man," the guard said.

Carter slumped back. "I see."

Josepsson came in a minute or two later; he seemed flustered.

"What have you done, you madman?" he shouted. He hurried across the room and slapped Carter's face.

Carter reached out and grabbed the man by the throat and pulled him down. It had been too quick for the two guards. They started forward.

"Another step and I break his neck," Carter shouted.

Both men hesitated.

Josepsson's face was turning red. He was struggling, but to no avail.

"Back to the door," Carter said. "I'll kill him otherwise. Long before you could reach me, I'd break his neck."

They stepped back after a moment, and Carter got to his feet, pushing the Icelander back.

"Who do you work for?" Carter asked the two guards.

Their eyes narrowed. "Mr. Josepsson."

"You're his personal bodyguards?" Carter asked. "Is that it?"

"No . . . we work for the Icelandic Internal Security Division."

"What about Ziegler?"

"What about him?"

"Do you take orders from him?"

"Of course not," one of the guards said.

Carter looked at Josepsson. He was probably making a very large mistake, but he could not fight an entire country. He suspected, as did Hawk, that Josepsson had either been blackmailed by Ziegler or had been completely taken in by the man. Now that they had come this far, it was too late for Josepsson to get out.

Carter let him go and shoved him back. Then he sat down and crossed his legs.

The guards had leaped forward, their guns at the ready, but Josepsson held them back.

"Very good," Carter said. "Now why don't we all sit down and have a nice little chat. There is a lot I have to tell you."

"What are you doing here, Mr. Carter?" Josepsson asked, rubbing his neck. He stepped back and leaned against the desk.

"A cigarette," Carter said, carefully digging out his pack and his lighter. The guards watched his every movement. When he had it lit, he looked at Josepsson. "I came up here originally to find out what happened to a very dear friend of mine."

"Dr. Coatsworth."

"Yes. Ziegler's people—your people—killed her."

Josepsson winced. "I had nothing to do with it."

"I came up here this time to destroy your nuclear generator and processing plant."

"Did your government send you?" Josepsson snarled. There was little love lost between most Icelanders and the U.S.

"No," Carter said. Any AXE mission anywhere in the world was always denied. It was one of the ways in which the agency was kept sacrosanct.

"Then why . . . what have you got against—"

"Your friend General Ziegler is building more than a nuclear power plant. He's also building a spent fuel re-processing plant."

"Yes, to make new fuel rods."

Carter shook his head. "No. The reprocessing plant will make nuclear bomb material."

"That's insanity," Josepsson shouted, straightening up.

"Not only that, but General Ziegler is a very high-ranking member of the Odessa," Carter said. "You have heard of that organization, haven't you?"

"Impossible," Josepsson said. But he was losing his conviction. "Inconceivable."

Carter looked around. "Is this your house?"

Josepsson nodded.

"Ziegler is your house guest?"

Again Josepsson nodded.

"Fine. Let's wait until he returns—I assume you told him that you had me—and see what he has to say."

"He's on his way out here now. He said he has something very important to say to me. Something to explain. Something vital to Iceland's future."

"Very vital to your country's future. I just wonder if you are ready to hear about it."

Josepsson just looked at him but said nothing. The two guards seemed worried.

THIRTEEN

The sun shone in the barracks windows, and Roberta squinted up against the brightness as the door shut behind the guard, and she was alone for a moment. Every bone and muscle in her body was on fire from where she had been beaten. Eight men had raped her so far, each one stronger and more violent than the last.

She had finally stopped fighting them, and it had made it easier, although no less endurable. She wanted to roll over and die, here and now. Except for the thought of Ziegler, she would have given up. But somehow, somewhere, at some time, she knew she would see him dead.

As she lay there she expected the door to open at any moment and another of Ziegler's guards to come in for her. But as the minutes passed and no one came, she began to hope they had had enough for a while. Just a little while, she told herself. She needed rest.

The had not really hurt her, not physically and not badly. She would be bruised a bit, but there were no broken bones, no torn flesh or muscles. Just the shame and filth of it all. It made her shudder.

She rolled over. Her breasts ached from where the men had pawed at her, and the muscles in her thighs were shaking. She was sick to her stomach.

"Oh, Nick," she cried softly, the tears coming easily to

her eyes. If they had caught and killed him, it could be some time before Schmidt followed this up. She could be here like this for days, perhaps weeks.

How in God's name had her mother endured it all those months? The pain, the misery, the humiliation?

Her thoughts kept going around in circles from Ziegler to her mother to Nick Carter and back to Ziegler.

And this was only the first day, she told herself as she drifted off to sleep.

Someone was at the door. She woke, her heart suddenly thumping in her chest, her stomach heaving. For a moment or two she was confused about what was happening. But it sounded like someone scuffling outside her door.

"Nick?" she called out softly.

There was a dull thump against the wall, and Roberta pushed herself up. Someone called out softly, then she heard the unmistakable popping sound of a silenced pistol shot. The lock splintered, and the door was shoved open.

God, she thought, it was about to happen again. She was still confused.

Two men, both wearing hard hats and both dressed in the gray coveralls everyone in the compound wore, leaped into the room.

"Roberta Redgrave?" one of them asked in German. His voice held a strange accent.

Roberta managed to nod.

Then he was beside her while the other man pulled a body into the room and shut the door. He proceeded to strip the man's coveralls and boots.

"Are you all right?" the man who came in first asked Roberta. She looked up into his eyes. They were hard, but they had the look of a friend.

She nodded. "Bruised. But I think I can walk."

"Good," the man said.

"Who are you?"

"Hold on," he said. He took the fallen guard's coveralls from the other man, and he quickly dressed her in them. In a couple of minutes he had put the too-large boots on her feet, laced them up, and pulled her off the bed.

She was dizzy, and she had to lean on him for support.

"Sure you're all right? We can carry you."

"I'm walking out of here on my own steam," she insisted. "Now just who the hell are you, and where's Nick Carter?"

The other one was at the door. He turned back. "You don't know us. But a man by the name of Roger Seidman sent us."

"Seidman?" The name was vaguely familiar.

"That's right. Israeli embassy. Buenos Aires."

"Oh, my God," Roberta breathed. "You're Mossad."

"I'm Ari," the one holding her said.

"I'm Paul," the one by the door added. "But we're all going to be dead unless we get out of here right now."

"How . . ." Roberta asked, but Ari held her off.

"Let's save the explanations for later. I'd like to get out of here first."

"Let's go," Paul said. He threw open the door and hurried out, with Ari and a not-too-steady Roberta right behind him.

There were two bodies in the corridor, and another one lay in the barracks day room. Just outside was a military jeep, its top up, its side curtains zippered.

There was a lot of traffic up and down the dirt road; the maintenance crews working on the burned-out barracks and the remains of the motor pool, which was still smoldering across the compound.

No one paid them any attention as they ducked out of the barracks and climbed into the jeep, Paul behind the wheel, Ari in the passenger seat, and Roberta seated low in the back.

Ari handed her back an Uzi submachine gun as Paul took off down the main road toward the front gate. She unfolded the wire stock and checked to make sure the big clip was seated properly, and that a round was in the firing chamber.

"I don't have to ask if you know how to use that," Ari said. "But just be ready if we have to shoot our way out of here."

"Where's Nick, and how the hell did you get from Buenos

Aires to here?'' Roberta demanded. Now that she was moving again, the strength was coming back to her.

"Your Mr. Carter came to our embassy in Buenos Aires last week asking questions about General Ziegler. We had been watching him for several years.''

"I worked for him,'' Roberta said.

"We know,'' Paul replied, glancing over his shoulder. They were almost to the main gate. "And we weren't overly surprised when Mr. Carter and you got together.''

"Our boss told us to keep tabs on both of you,'' Ari said.

"Germany? Washington?''

"That's right. Then here, although we nearly lost you a couple of times.'' Ari turned forward as they approached the gate. He had an Uzi on his lap. "Heads up,'' he said.

They slowed down as they approached the guardhouse, and two men with automatic weapons stepped out on the road.

"They don't look too friendly,'' Paul said.

"Not at all,'' Ari replied. He shoved the side flap aside, slammed the bolt back on the submachine gun, and stuck it out the window as Paul gunned the jeep.

One of the guards went down; the other leaped to the left as the jeep hit the weakened gate and crashed through.

Roberta had turned around in her seat, and as the second guard jumped up and started to bring his weapon to bear, she fired out the back plastic window, the sound incredibly loud in the confines of the jeep. The guard never had a chance.

"Nice shot,'' Ari said as they hauled down the road, the jeep's engine winding out in each gear. At the main highway Paul barely slowed down as he turned toward Reykjavik, but the going became much easier on the pavement.

"You okay back there?'' Paul said.

"Just fine,'' Roberta replied. She made sure the safety was on, and she folded up the Uzi's stock and put the weapon aside. "Now how did you know where to find me?''

"We followed you and Carter out here last night. After the explosions, he took off through the main gate in a big truck.

In the confusion we walked in and have been working there all night.'' Ari hesitated a moment. ''Everyone was talking about . . . you,'' he said delicately.

''Then you don't know what happened to Nick?''

''We assume he went back into town,'' Paul said.

Roberta looked back the way they had come. ''And Ziegler?''

''He left an hour or so ago,'' Ari said. ''I watched him drive out the main gate. It looked as if he was in a big hurry.''

Roberta was still slightly dazed. She tried to think this out. ''Nick has gone back to the hotel. I was supposed to return there last night as soon as he was through the fence.''

''Instead you had to play tricks with the gate guards,'' Ari said.

''I want Ziegler,'' she flared.

Ari turned around. ''Who does Carter work for?''

Roberta shook her head. ''I don't know . . . for sure. One of the U.S. intelligence services. Probably the State Department.''

''Does he know about your mother? What happened between her and Ziegler during the war?''

The color drained from Roberta's face. ''My . . . mother. . . ?''

''We know about it. Does Carter?''

She started to say no, a mist in her eyes and a thickness in her throat, but then she thought about the note she had left for him back at the hotel, and she nodded. ''By now he does,'' she managed.

''I see,'' Ari said, and they drove the rest of the way into Reykjavik in silence.

They entered the hotel by the back way, and only one of the maids saw them. The woman raised her eyebrows at Roberta's too-large coveralls and boots, but she had seen a lot of things in her day, so she continued with her work.

The note was gone from beneath the pillow, but that was the only indication that Carter had been here.

''Where else could he have gone?'' Ari asked.

Roberta stood in the middle of the room. "Back to the compound, or . . ."

"Or?" Ari asked.

"Where does Ziegler stay when he's in Iceland? Do you know?"

"Here in Reykjavik—or just outside the city. He's a house guest of Thorstein Josepsson."

"Josepsson," Roberta said. "He mentioned the name."

"Do you think he could have gone out there?"

"Possibly."

"But why? Or do you think he might have known where Ziegler was staying?"

"He might have," Roberta said. "He didn't tell me everything."

"Get cleaned up and changed," Paul said. "We'll drive out there and take a look."

The study door burst open and General Marc Ziegler strode in imperiously, his nostrils flared, a slight sheen of perspiration on his forehead as if he had been running.

"So, Herr Carter, we meet again. This time you will not wander off so easily," he said. He pulled out Carter's old Luger. "I understand you somehow came up with another of these. Clever."

Josepsson, who had been seated on the couch drinking coffee, jumped up. "I demand some explanations," he said. "Now. This morning."

Ziegler looked at him with some amusement. "And you shall have them, my dear Thorstein. But whatever this man has been filling your head with is nonsense, I can assure you."

"I certainly hope so," Josepsson said. Carter could hear a note of relief in his voice.

Ziegler looked over his shoulder at Josepsson's two men. "Go have some breakfast. We'll call you if we need you."

They hesitated, but after a moment Josepsson motioned for

them to go ahead, and they left the study, softly closing the door behind them.

"Now, if you will be so good as to pour me some of that coffee, we can begin," Ziegler said. He came across and took a seat directly across from Carter.

"I understand you had a little trouble last night out at the reactor site," Carter said, smiling.

Ziegler's jaws tightened momentarily, but then he returned the smile. "Only a minor setback, I assure you. Nothing serious was damaged."

"Thank God for that," Josepsson said, pouring the coffee. "We can't afford a delay at this point."

"But tell me," Carter said. "Now that we're at this point, why was Lydia Coatsworth murdered?"

"She wasn't . . ." Josepsson started, but Ziegler interrupted him.

"Because she discovered our pumping plant. She had to be eliminated."

"Her body was moved?"

"Yes. We put her in a plastic bag and packed ice around her."

"But I thought it was an accident," Josepsson said, his voice wavering.

"Shut up, you old woman," Ziegler snapped, the Luger vacillating between him and Carter.

"What pumping plant?" Carter asked. It was all he could do to keep himself in control.

"Alpha," Ziegler said smugly. "It's the cornerstone of the entire project. We're tapping off geothermal energy from the Reykjavik field. The university geologists all figured it was the end of Iceland's unlimited free energy. Or at least they were coming to that consensus until that bitch Coatsworth stuck her nose into our business. She died for it. Just like you will, Carter." Ziegler laughed. "But your girlfriend, Roberta, she's a different story."

Carter could feel his muscles tensing. Roberta had evidently been captured out at the compound. She had made a try on Ziegler and it had failed. Just as he had failed with the plastique.

"Who is this, now?" Josepsson chirped. "Another woman? Who is she?"

"She used to be my secretary in Buenos Aires. But she is another spy."

"The killing has to stop. I can no longer be a party to this kind of—"

"Then go. Take your pretty boys with you and get out of here. I'll give you a few minutes to get away so that you can have your alibi," Ziegler snapped.

"You mean to kill this man?"

"That's right."

Josepsson looked at Carter, put the coffee cup down, then hurried across the room and left.

"He is a weak man," Ziegler said. "Although necessary. While you, on the other hand, are apparently a very strong man and totally unnecessary."

"What have you done with Roberta?" Carter asked evenly.

"The same thing I did to her mother."

"You're pretty good when it comes to women. How about men?"

Ziegler chuckled. "Physically I'm no match for you, young man. I have no illusions about my strength. But as far as intelligence goes . . ."

"I would have thought your arm was stronger than your brain by the way you've botched things up here."

Ziegler was still smiling, although it looked as if his humor was wearing thin. "Everything's on schedule. Even your little display of pyrotechnics last night did nothing but slow us down by a few days."

"I'm not talking about that, Herr General. I'm talking about Lydia Coatsworth, who worked for the Central Intelligence Agency," he lied, "and about Roberta Redgrave, who works for the West German BND. And there are several others on their way up here.''

Ziegler did not seem quite so sure of himself now. ''And you?''

''You'll never know . . .'' Carter said, and his eyes suddenly went wide as he looked beyond Ziegler. ''Holy. . . !''

Ziegler started to turn, and Carter spun left off the chair while grabbing for his stiletto in its chamois case on his left forearm.

Ziegler fired once, the bullet lodging in the floor where Carter's legs had been a moment before, and then he stepped back.

Carter leaped on Ziegler before he could get off another shot, driving the stiletto upward into his chest between his ribs, piercing his heart.

The German cried out, then fell backward out of Carter's arms. He was dead.

Carter snatched the Luger and went to the door. He eased it open a crack, half expecting Josepsson's two giants to be there. But there was nothing. Absolutely nothing. The house was deathly still. Josepsson and his two goons had apparently left.

He retrieved his stiletto from Ziegler's body, wiped the blade clean, then took the man's car keys from his pocket and headed out.

Evidently, Roberta was still back at the compound. He was going to have to free her and then finish what he had come here to do in the first place.

FOURTEEN

"Five will get you ten that Josepsson is on his way to meet Ziegler," Paul said.

"But this is the opposite direction of the reactor site," Ari said.

They had just reached Josepsson's place when the man stormed out of his house accompanied by two huge, blond men, climbed into his car, and drove off to the south.

Paul kept well back so that they would not be noticed, but the farther south they drove, the less traffic there was and the more likely it became that they'd be spotted.

Roberta was beside herself with fear for Carter's safety. She was convinced he had gone back out to the compound to rescue her. Balancing that concern, however, was the possibility that Josepsson would lead them to Ziegler, and she would have another chance at the general. She could envision the man in the sights of the Uzi. She'd empty an entire clip into the son of a bitch's body.

"Are you all right?" Ari asked.

She looked up, realizing she had been shaking. "I will be as soon as we take care of Ziegler and find Nick."

The countryside south of the city was very flat at first, not beginning to rise up into the volcanic slag heaps and hills for at least another twenty miles.

Josepsson's car continued out ahead of them, and after a

while Roberta wondered if the man was intending on driving all the way across the country.

"It's just possible that he's making his escape," Ari said after a long time of silence.

"Because of the trouble out at the site last night?" Paul asked.

"Could be he's frightened. Realized that he's in far over his head. He might even have found out, somehow, just what Ziegler and his gang are really up to, and it's much more than he bargained for."

"Do you think so?" Roberta asked from the back seat.

Ari shrugged. "It's possible . . ." he started to say, but then he sat up. "Here we go."

Josepsson's car had turned off the main highway and was heading across a rock-strewn cinder field toward a pair of mounds on the horizon.

Paul slowed down until the Icelander's car had topped the rise and had disappeared on the other side. Then it sped up again, turning off the highway and following the same track.

"You'd better stop before we get to the top," Ari said. "No telling how quickly he pulled up over on the other side."

Paul nodded, and just before the crest of the hill, he brought the car to a halt. All three of them jumped out, Uzi submachine guns in hand, and hurried the rest of the way to the top on foot.

Josepsson's car was nowhere in sight. But the dirt track led off to the right about two hundred and fifty yards, going between two mounds that looked like the breasts of a gigantic woman lying back.

"Roberta and I will have a look-see," Ari said to Paul, "while you bring up the car."

"No heroics," Paul said, and he went back to the car as Ari and Roberta headed down the dirt track that Josepsson's car had to have followed.

Paul was just coming over the crest of the hill when she and Ari rounded the curve. She had expected to see the road continuing off into the distance. Instead, across the far side of the mound was a large steel door, almost like an air raid shelter. It was open.

One of Josepsson's gigantic men popped out from below and immediately opened fire.

Ari raised the Uzi and fired from the hip, catching the man in the chest, spinning him around and back inside.

Paul came up with the car, jumped out, and raced over to them.

"What happened?"

"One of Josepsson's guys," Ari said.

The three of them approached the open door cautiously. Josepsson's man lay dead on the floor of a very large, immaculately clean room. Valves and dial faces adorned the far wall. A door off to the left was open, the sound of heavy machinery running very loud now.

Ari motioned for Paul to take the right side of the door while he and Roberta took the left. Weapons at the ready, they raced across the control room and looked down.

The door opened onto a catwalk that looked down into a two-story-deep room filled with a maze of multicolored pipes, valves, and other equipment. It was very hot here, and the noise of the machinery seemed to be changing pitch . . . to a much deeper, almost off-key rumbling.

The other bodyguard trotted into view below, and when he spotted them up on the catwalk, he ducked back out of sight. They returned to the control room.

"Josepsson," Ari shouted down, but his voice was lost to the noise.

The bodyguard came back around the pipes, fired several shots up at the doorway, the slugs ricocheting off the metal catwalk. Then he ran to the bottom of the stairs and started up.

Ari turned through the doorway and fired a burst down the stairs, making a bloody pulp of the man's chest, sending him tumbling backward down the stairs.

A second later Josepsson came running around the corner,

waving them away and shouting something they could not hear. Ari almost shot him until he realized the man was not armed.

Josepsson got about five paces away from the corner joints of a mass of pipes when the machinery noise suddenly exploded into a cacophony of explosions, high-pitched screams, and discordant rumblings. The Icelander was engulfed in a tremendous billow of high-pressure, superheated steam, dying instantly.

"This place is going to blow!" Ari shouted, his voice all but lost. "They must have overloaded the pumps!"

They scrambled back away from the doorway, raced through the main door outside, and got to the jeep just as the ground underfoot began to shake ominously.

Paul had the jeep started as Roberta leaped in the back seat, and he spun it around in a tight circle and headed away as fast as he could shift through the gears.

They just made it over the crest of the hill when an ear-splitting explosion shattered the morning stillness, both mounds behind them rising straight up.

Whatever had been down there was not there any longer, but all that Roberta could think about was Nick Carter, whom she was convinced now had returned to the reactor site to finish the job he had set out to do, and to rescue her.

Ziegler's car was a very large, dark Cadillac limousine. Carter started it and brought it around to the front of the house. He opened the rear car door, then went inside to the study and returned carrying Ziegler's body. He propped the body up in one corner of the back seat, strapped a seat belt around him, then headed back through Reykjavik and out to the reactor site.

At least Roberta wasn't dead yet. He had learned that much from Ziegler. Beyond that meager information he had no idea where she was or in what condition she might be in.

But he damned well was going to find out, and anyone who got in his way would be dead. Instantly.

With his Luger on the seat next to him, Carter accelerated out of town, and soon he was doing better than a hundred miles an hour down the narrow, blacktopped road. In his mind was nothing but a single direction, a single operation. And when it was finished, either he would be dead or a lot of others would be if they got in the way.

At that speed, he made it out to the turnoff in less than an hour, and he didn't slow down very much as he barreled down the dirt road, the car's heavy-duty springs bottoming out several times on the ruts.

When he came within sight of the front gate, however, he slowed down and checked in the back to make sure Ziegler's body hadn't fallen over; the general looked like a tired man staring out the window on the opposite side, lost in thought.

Carter stopped just at the gate, and the guards, recognizing the car, swung the shaky barrier open and waved them through. Carter waved back as he passed, then half turned and opened and closed his mouth as if he were talking to Ziegler.

The ruse worked, and he drove up to what he took to be the administration center, where he went behind the building to the parking area and pulled up next to a truck.

There was a lot of activity on the site today, but no one noticed as Carter reached back, unstrapped the seat belt holding Ziegler's body, and pushed it over down onto the floor, out of sight.

Pocketing his Luger, Carter got out of the car, went across the parking area, and entered the building. The place was humming with activity, and Carter stopped the first man he passed.

"Is General Ziegler's secretary still here?" he asked.

"Of course," the harried man snapped. He pointed down the corridor to the left. "She's in her office, I assume." Then he was gone.

Carter hurried down the corridor and into the reception area. A young woman was seated at a desk. "Is General Ziegler's secretary in?"

"Yes," she said. "Just through there." She pointed over her shoulder and looked up. "But the general isn't here."

"I know that," Carter said. He went around her desk and entered the general's outer office without knocking. A man in coveralls was seated on the desk, talking with a young, blond woman. They both looked up when Carter came in. The man jumped up.

"Can I help you?" he said.

Carter closed the door behind him and pulled out his Luger. "For your sake you'd better hope so," he said.

The man stepped back, nearly falling over the desk.

"Oh," the young woman said.

"There was a woman here. General Ziegler has her. Where is she?"

The man hesitated.

Carter raised the Luger and flipped the safety off. The man blanched.

"She was here. But she's gone. Two men took her."

"You're lying!" Carter snapped.

"No. I swear it. Two of them got in the compound somehow. They killed four of our people. They're gone."

"When?"

"Hours ago."

Carter didn't think he was lying. There was no reason for it. He stepped aside and motioned toward the door with his gun. "Let's go."

"Where?" the woman asked.

"For a ride. I have the general's car outside." He pocketed the gun but kept his hand on the butt, his finger curled around the trigger. "I will not hesitate to kill you if either of you makes the slightest false move. Do you understand?"

The girl and the man nodded as they edged around the desk to the door.

"If anyone asks where you're going, we've been summoned by the general."

The man nodded, and Carter motioned for the door. They all went out. No one challenged them as they went down the corridor and out the back door.

"You can drive," Carter said to the man. "You next to him," he instructed the girl. He wanted them both up front, because he had no idea how they would react if they saw Ziegler's body.

"You're the one who was here last night . . . setting the explosions," the man said. Carter gave him the keys, and he started the car.

"That's right. Only now you're going to help me finish the job. And if you both behave, you won't get hurt."

"But General Ziegler . . ." the girl started.

"He's gone. He won't be back," Carter snapped. "Let's go."

The man backed out of the parking area, and Carter directed him further within the compound to the small shed that contained the dynamite. They backed up to the door.

Carter took the keys, and he and the man got out.

"If you run, miss, I'll come after you and kill you. If you stay here and behave yourself, you'll live through this."

"Yes, sir," the frightened woman said.

Carter opened the trunk, and he and the workman loaded it with four boxes of the dynamite. Then they closed the trunk lid.

Back in the car, Carter directed the man back to the construction road, and they headed up the hill to the reactor building.

"You can't do this," the workman said.

"Yes, I can, and I will," Carter said. "Stop the car."

The workman complied. They were still several hundred yards around from the reactor core control support.

"Out. Both of you. And you'd better run like hell away from here, because within a couple of minutes there's going to be one hell of an explosion."

The man and woman leaped out of the car and headed directly across the rock-strewn field as Carter climbed behind the wheel and took off up the hill to the reactor core support.

The big car slewed around in the gravel at the base of the massive concrete support, and Carter jumped out, opened the trunk, and began piling the cases of dynamite against it.

Two guards came around the corner. "Hey! What the hell are you doing?" one of them shouted.

Carter pulled out his Luger and fired three shots, both men going down. He stacked the fourth case against the base of the support, then jumped back into the car and raced off down the hill.

The compound siren began to wail as Carter pulled up behind a huge earthmover a hundred yards down from the core support base, jumped out of the car, and hurried around so that he had a clear sight line to the dynamite. From this distance he could barely make out the stacked-up boxes, but he drew out his Luger, got down on one knee, steadied the weapon in the classic shooter's position, and squeezed off the first shot.

A puff of concrete dust rose from the core support a couple of feet above the boxes. He lowered his aim and squeezed off two shots, both low.

Other sirens were wailing now, and the dirt began kicking up around Carter. They were shooting at him.

Oblivious to that, he raised his aim, held his breath, and delicately squeezed off a fourth shot. Almost at the same instant the Luger fired, the dynamite exploded in a tremendous roar. Carter just managed to scramble back behind the huge earthmover when huge chunks of concrete, some of them larger than a car, began raining down from the sky.

He ducked beneath the machine as the hunks of concrete and metal reinforcing rods slammed into the car.

Gradually the debris stopped falling, and Carter scrambled out from beneath the earthmover and climbed back into the incredibly battered car that looked as if it had fallen off a mountain.

It started and drove all right, however, and within seconds he was careening down the road, dodging the larger chunks of fallen concrete, to the main gate, which was half open.

He was racing down the dirt road toward the highway when he spotted the jeep coming his way.

He pressed harder on the accelerator, but as he passed the jeep he caught just a glimpse of Roberta.

He slammed on the brakes, made a skidding U-turn, and started back at the same time the jeep headed toward him.

They stopped together. "Nick! Nick!" Roberta screamed, leaping out of the jeep.

Carter had his Luger at the ready as she fell sobbing into his arms.

"We're friends, Mr. Carter," Ari said.

"He's telling the truth, Nick!" Roberta screamed. "They saved my life."

"We've got a Lear jet on the other side of Reykjavik. I think it'd be wise if we got the hell out of here."

"I'll drive," Carter said, and they all piled into Ziegler's battered Cadillac, Roberta staring down at Ziegler's body.

The western shores of Iceland dropped away as the Lear jet headed up into the perfectly clear blue sky. Paul Ahrens was in the left seat, and Ari Ben Shamonn was in the right. Roberta had gone back into the cabin to rest, while Carter talked with the two Mossad agents.

"You've been following us since Buenos Aires?" Carter was saying.

"On and off. You lost us in Germany."

"And in Washington?"

"We missed you there, too. We were doing our homework. Although we did trace you and the girl to your apartment."

Ari looked at his watch. "We've got a five-hour flight ahead of us. You might want some rest."

"Washington?"

"New York," Paul said. "You'll have to make it the rest of the way on your own, although if you get the chance, and your boss—whoever he is—gives you the go-ahead, we'd like a report."

"I think that can be arranged."

Ari looked at Carter. "It would have been better if Ziegler had lived to stand trial, but I'm glad it happened the way it did."

"Yeah," Carter said. "Me too."

He turned and went back into the Lear's main cabin. The plastic windowshades had been drawn, and the cabin was in semidarkness. For a moment or two he couldn't see a thing.

"Close the cockpit door, Nick," Roberta called out to him.

He did, and when he turned back he began to make out Roberta's form. She had made up the small bed, and she was lying there, fully clothed.

"Hold me," she said. "Please."

He kicked off his boots and went back to her. It'd be a while before she'd be able to forget what had happened to her. Until then, or at least until the pain eased for her, he'd stick close . . . very close.

DON'T MISS THE NEXT NEW
NICK CARTER SPY THRILLER

THE BUDAPEST RUN

The staccato chattering of Michaels' submachine gun from the top of the stairs was like a single explosion in Carter's ears. His hand lifted from the doorknob as if it had touched fire.

Michaels had come through. Carter had little doubt now that the man had done his job like a pro. He also surmised that no matter how many were trying to get into the tower room, none of them would be successful.

As if in answer to his thoughts, there was an agonizing scream of pain and the sound of a body falling down the stairs. Almost at the same time the firing stopped.

''Back,'' Dontaine replied, already backing away down the corridor.

Carter threw the switch on his penlight to full, ripped off the shield that had narrowed its beam and sat it on the floor. Dontaine followed his lead so that the door was now awash with light.

Both men retreated another few paces and crouched to wait.

It was a short wait.

The man Carter remembered as the chief orderly, Goetz, burst through the door first with the stumpy Nedda Alfree close behind, Goetz' left arm hung useless at his side, a bloody mess.

Both he and Nedda Alfree carried Mausers.

As they hit the light, their reactions were very different. Nedda threw her hands up to shield her eyes from the glare.

Goetz screamed with rage and began firing wildly down the corridor.

Carter and Dontaine fired simultaneously.

Goetz seemed to explode as if a bomb had gone off deep in his guts. He buckled and began to fall forward. To both Carter's and Dontaine's surprise, Nedda Alfree proved more adept than they imagined. She reached out and caught the falling man. Then, using just the strength of one arm, she held him in front of her like a shield.

With more strength than most men, Nedda drove directly toward the two men, hurtling Goetz before her, the Mauser barking from her right hand.

"Look out," Dontaine cried, getting off two shots that thudded into the already lifeless body.

At the last second she hurled the body at Carter and turned to fire twice at Dontaine's huddled form.

Carter tried to evade but it was hopeless. He went down under the big orderly's bulk. By the time he had squirmed free the woman was almost at the junction of the hallways.

"Stop, Nedda!" Nick shouted, dropping to one knee, "or else . . ."

—From *The Budapest Run*
A New Nick Carter Spy Thriller
From Charter in December

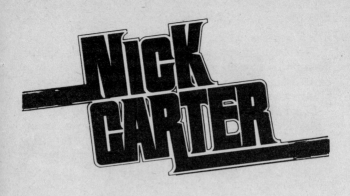

NICK CARTER

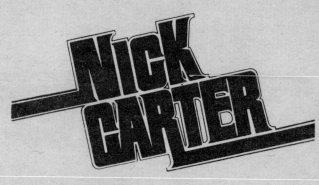

NICK CARTER

☐ 71539-7	**RETREAT FOR DEATH**	$2.50
☐ 75035-4	**THE SATAN TRAP**	$1.95
☐ 76347-2	**THE SIGN OF THE COBRA**	$2.25
☐ 77193-9	**THE SNAKE FLAG CONSPIRACY**	$2.25
☐ 77413-X	**SOLAR MENACE**	$2.50
☐ 79073-9	**THE STRONTIUM CODE**	$2.50
☐ 79077-1	**THE SUICIDE SEAT**	$2.25
☐ 81025-X	**TIME CLOCK OF DEATH**	$1.75
☐ 82407-2	**TRIPLE CROSS**	$1.95
☐ 82726-8	**TURKISH BLOODBATH**	$2.25
☐ 87192-5	**WAR FROMTHE CLOUDS**	$2.25

Available at your local bookstore or return this form to:

 CHARTER BOOKS
Book Mailing Service
P.O. Box 690, Rockville Centre, NY 11571

Please send me the titles checked above. I enclose _____ Include 75¢ for postage
and handling if one book is ordered; 25¢ per book for two or more not to exceed
$1.75. California, Illinois, New York and Tennessee residents please add sales tax.

NAME_____

ADDRESS_____

CITY_____STATE/ZIP_____

(allow six weeks for delivery.)   A8